EVERYONE **DIES**

A COLLECTION OF DARK TALES

EVERYONE **DIES**

A COLLECTION OF DARK TALES

JEAN DAVIS

Also by Jean Davis

Destiny Pills & Space Wizards
Sahmara
A Broken Race
The Last God
Dreams of Stars and Lies
Not Another Bard's Tale
Spindelkin

The Narvan
Trust
The Minor Years
Chain of Gray
Bound In Blue
Seeker

CONTENTS

MARBLE

Seven-year-old Sally Harper slipped out of her sleeping bag and pulled her mother's sweatshirt over her pajamas. She scrunched the long sleeves up over her thin arms. Someday, she'd grow into it, she hoped, and be as pretty has her mother had been before she'd gotten sick. Sally felt for the zipper of the tent flap and then pulled down slowly. Inch by inch, she held her breath.

Off in the distance, her father and his girlfriend, Beth, talked by the fire, sparks flickering up in the darkness. Sally felt for the flashlight in her pocket, assuring herself that it was where she'd tucked it earlier. Stars twinkled overhead as she searched for the racing light of a meteor. Maybe it was too early yet. Dad said they wouldn't be in the sky until long after bedtime.

She was seven, stupid Beth, and yes, she was perfectly old enough to stay up and watch the meteor shower. Sally stuck out her tongue in the direction of the fire. They just wanted to be alone, wanted her out of the way so they could do date stuff. Gross.

Sally glanced back at the tent flap hanging open. Beth would yell at her for letting bugs in if she didn't close it and if they glanced back and saw it open, they'd know she was up long after bedtime. There would be yelling about that too. She carefully worked the zipper back down to the dewy grass and wiped her wet hands on her pajama pants.

As she crept past the picnic table, firelight caught a half-full wine bottle next to an empty one. The marshmallow bag was still open and sitting out from when they'd toasted them earlier. She snuck three out of the bag and slipped them into her other pocket. If Dad wanted alone time with Beth, he'd get it. She would find somewhere else to watch the meteor shower.

Sally eyed the scattered pine trees and the rocky field of their off-road rustic campsite. Stupid Beth had thought it was romantic even though it didn't have a real bathroom. They'd been driving around in the truck, the three of them crammed into the front seat, her between them as they made silly faces at each other, for four days now. When would this vacation be over? The only good thing about it was the meteor shower and that being in Michigan's Upper Peninsula, where there was a whole lot of nothing but trees and rocks and more trees, the sky was really dark. She could see more stars than she'd ever seen from their backyard.

Glancing over her shoulder, she saw the silhouette of her dad kissing Beth. They weren't even watching for meteors. That was the whole point of being here! Filled with disgust, Sally marched through the trees toward higher ground where she could get a better view far away from the moany-groany sounds by the fire.

She clutched the flashlight but didn't dare use it for fear she might be seen. The twinkling stars offered just enough light that she could pick her way through the field of tall grass. By the third time she'd stubbed her toes on a hidden rock, she decided she'd gone far enough. The scattered trees hid most of the view below, but she could still pick out the light of the fire to make her way back later.

Sally settled in with her back against a big rock, tipping her head to rest on the top of it to gaze at the night sky. She could see all the way around her, the stars going on forever. The longer she stared at the tiny lights, the more of them she could see. It was beautiful, she thought to herself as she popped a stolen marshmallow into her mouth. The most beautiful thing she'd ever seen.

A thin blaze of light arced across the sky. She gasped. A real meteor. And Dad and Beth were missing it.

Minutes later, two more sped overhead. And then another. Sally grinned, chewing on her second marshmallow. She didn't dare blink for fear of missing the show.

They came in twos and threes, racing across the sky. Sometimes they were close together, sometimes like strangers going to the same place but keeping their distance. Her imagination ran wild, wondering if the lights ever reached the ground and what they might do there, or if they continued onward, racing through the sky forever.

She reached for her last snack but her fingers fumbled as she pulled it from the large pocket. The marshmallow fell into the grass. Sally felt around, but couldn't find it. She tore her gaze from the sky and slipped the flashlight into her hand, pulling it up into her sleeve to keep the shining light dim. She'd just located the missing marshmallow when the light seemed to grow impossibly brighter. Dad was sure to notice. Panicked, she turned off the flashlight. The light still grew brighter. Her father must be using the big light he kept in his truck to search for her. Sally huddled beside the rock, hoping to hide until she could make a run for the tent. If she could make it back to her sleeping bag, she wouldn't get in trouble.

Her heart pounded. The light was so bright it made her eyes hurt. She looked up, expecting to see her father's angry face, but instead, the light swallowed her. A deafening explosion rocked the ground. She clamped her hands over her ears, but it was too late. The sound filled her head, echoing, pounding over and over until she thought her head would explode.

Surrounded by searing heat, Sally tried to scream but no sound came out. Her skin bubbled and blackened. She squeezed her eyes shut, not knowing if she even had eyes anymore. Everything was black.

And then suddenly, it wasn't.

Sally opened her eyes. Her eyelids felt odd, odd in a way that she'd never noticed the feeling of her eyelids until just then. They were dry like paper, crunchy feeling. The heat she'd felt before was no longer painful but kept her warm like she'd been playing in the sand at the beach all day. She held out a hand, marveling at her blackened skin, cracked and bleeding, but without any pain. Tattered remnants of her mother's sweatshirt and her pajamas had melted onto her flesh, becoming one with her cooling lava skin. That's what it reminded her of, like one of the nature movies they'd had to watch in school. Cooling lava. Black on the outside, red-hot on the inside.

The thundering explosion had faded from her ears and now she could hear her father calling for her. Beth's shrill voice yelled her name from farther away. Sally called out, but her voice was muffled like she had a mouth full of marshmallows. Warm liquid dribbled from her lips. She reached up and wiped it away.

As she took a step toward her father's voice, her foot knocked into a cracked, hollow stone. The inside glistened. Fascinated, she poked a finger inside the stone that was as big as the large marble from the set Beth had tried to teach her how to play. The stupid game had made her thumb hurt.

The liquid in the rock felt like the oil that leaked onto the driveway from her father's truck, kind of thick and smooth. Exactly like what had come out of her mouth.

Sally spun around, staring at the ground. The grass where she had been sitting, everything where she had been sitting looked like a fire pit, charred and smoking. She was smoking. Sally tried to scream, but again, no real sound came out, which made her want to scream all the more.

Maybe this was a bad dream. It had to be a bad dream, her mind telling her she'd been naughty for sneaking out of the tent. There was no way that her mother's sweatshirt could be ruined. That she could have been on fire.

She looked at the broken marble rock again and then at the deep dark trail of midnight blackness that ran between where the rock was and where she'd been sitting only a step away. They were as neatly connected as if she'd drawn the line with a pencil.

Her father's voice grew louder. Sally ran toward him. She couldn't bear to look at his face, knowing he would be mad that she'd snuck out. Instead, she aimed right for his waist and wrapped her arms around him, sobbing that she was sorry, tears flowing from her eyes.

The oily blackness soaked into his shirt. An awful smell filled the air. Sally backed away, thinking she might throw up. Her father let out a scream that made every muscle in Sally's body go tight. Beth, closer now, yelled both of their names.

Sally stood frozen as the blackness flowed over her father, burning every inch of him as it worked up from his waist and down to his boots. His hair fell away like ashes and his clothes burned like newspaper fed to a fire. In the space of three breaths, his skin glowed like embers. Black fluid ran from his mouth when he opened it. He held out his hands to Sally, shaking his head. Then he shook all over and fell to the ground.

The dewy grass around them caught fire, smoldering and smoking, filling the air with a dark haze. Beth burst through the heavy cloud and shrieked.

Sally watched as Beth ran to where her father lay huddled in the burning grass, trying to reach for him, crying wet, clear tears. Beth ripped off her sweatshirt and beat it on top of him, on the grass, on everything around her as she was now surrounded by the low, spreading fire. Sally noticed that with each step she took toward Beth, she left a black smoldering footstep. Fire ignited behind her.

Beth caught sight of Sally and shrieked. She shot to her feet, clutching her smoking sweatshirt, and backed away.

Sally glanced at her father. He wasn't moving anymore. Terrified, she ran for Beth. Beth would help her. She had to, didn't she?

Beth's eyes were cartoon-wide. She screamed

as Sally barreled forward. The faster Sally moved, the more orange sparks flew from her skin, falling like glitter beside and behind her, bursting into tiny flames as soon as they landed. She held out her hand, reaching for Beth, desperately wanting to hold the woman she'd been avoiding touching since her father had introduced them four months ago.

She tried to explain what had happened, to ask Beth to help her father, to plead for Beth to help her, but only mumbles came from her cracked lips. Greasy blackness dribbled down her chin. Her fingertips brushed Beth's arm, but then the woman who had said she wanted to be Sally's mother turned and ran.

As Sally ran after Beth, fire followed her, growing until the air crackled. Each tree and bush she passed burst into flame until the sky was filled with black smoke and flickering with an eerie orange light.

Sally's foot caught on something, sending her sprawling onto the ground. Struggling to get to her hands and knees, she noticed a black hand, a blackened arm. Beth lay in the grass, oily liquid burbling from her mouth as her skin took on an orange and black glow like little charcoal bricks in a grill.

Not knowing what else to do, Sally bolted for the truck. She stumbled, her legs tired, the air too hot to breathe. Slower now, she walked, each step a chore.

The tents were already smoking when she made it to the campsite. The fire in the little stone ring roared to life as she passed by. Her arm shook, but she managed to get the truck door open and crawl inside. She would be safe there, safe until someone came to help them.

Sally gazed out the window, watching the dancing flames eat the hillside and race outward, gobbling up everything it touched all around her. Her whole body started to shake.

The seat beneath her began to burn. Heavy black smoke filled the truck. Sally tried to open the door, but her hand was shaking too badly. Then it stopped working at all, her fingers curling in, the lava light going out. She cried black tears until the truck itself shook and the roar of the flames outside filled her last thoughts. The truck exploded, taking Sally with it as it spread the oily blackness into the sky where the wind deposited tiny drops for miles around. Flames consumed it all.

FOREVER

Stella stared up at the twinkling stars while Devon disposed of the remains of their late-night picnic in the park. "It's such a beautiful night. You're right. A date night is just what we needed."

Devon wiped his hands on his jeans and smiled. "No more parties. Just us. You and me forever, Stel."

She sighed. "I'll miss parties. And people. Not those last ones, obviously, but family and friends, you know?"

He took her hand, pulling her down onto the blanket next to him. "They won't understand us. It's better this way. For everyone."

"You're right. As usual." She kissed his cheek and rested her head on his shoulder.

Devon wrapped his arm around her, pulling her closer. Sitting here like this, she could almost pretend the attack had never happened, that the party two weeks ago hadn't changed their lives forever.

Leaves rustled in the warm summer breeze.

A swing creaked on the playset off to their left. Out here, in the middle of the park at this hour, no one would be looking for them. It wasn't like they had a car to announce their presence in the parking lot. Everything they owned was in the backpack beside the blanket that Devon carried when they'd walked under the cover of night.

They'd just wanted a fun night out. When the woman on the sidewalk had handed her a flyer, a night of music and dancing had seemed the perfect way to escape the disapproval of Stella's family and friends. They all said Devon was too old for her, too irresponsible, that he had too many tattoos, that he'd use her up, toss her aside and never look back. But here he was, taking care of her, providing for both of them, being responsible. When those goth assholes at the party had started harassing her, he hadn't hesitated to come to her defense. He hadn't thrown the first punch, but he'd put up a good fight before the seven sneering and stinking maniacs had dragged them both off into the shadows. That's where things had gotten really ugly, where she'd squeezed her eyes shut and screamed under the big, dirty hand clamped over her mouth. She'd never forget the wet slurping sounds and their low laughter.

Devon squeezed her hand. "You're doing it again. Don't think about it. They've moved on. They can't get us again. Not that they'd want us even if they did. They've already had their fun. This is our life now.

We're making the best of it, yeah?"

She nodded, doing her best to stamp out the vivid memories. A shooting star raced through the sky, pulling her attention back to the night they were supposed to be enjoying.

"Did you see it?" Devon asked.

"Yes. So beautiful. All of it. I don't remember there being so many stars before, do you?"

"No. Something good from the bad, yeah? Everything is more beautiful."

Good from the bad. He had a way of seeing that better than most people. Definitely better than her. Not for the first time, she wished she could explain this to her mother, that Devon wasn't the loser they'd labeled him. But Devon was right, it was just the two of them now. They didn't need anyone else. It *was* safer for everyone if they just stayed away, if who they had been died that night like the newspapers said. There had been a witness, some hysterical girl who claimed she'd seen their cold, drained corpses—which couldn't be true, because here they both were, watching the stars.

Stella did feel bad that the police were spending time looking for their bodies. Surely, they'd give up soon and everyone could get on with their lives.

"Where will we go next?" she asked

"Maybe up the coast? Wherever we want."

A branch snapped in the trees on the edge of the playground. Stella sat up, searching the shadows.

Devon shot to his feet beside her, scanning their surroundings.

"Ten of them, Stel. Can you hear them?"

She nodded as voices came into focus. Eight men and two women whispering in the woods. Improved hearing was good from the bad too, she supposed.

"Vampires spotted. Two, in the field," a man said.

Voices passed this information to one another until whispers surrounded Stella. As soft and beautiful as the night had been before, everything came into sharp focus now.

"Are you sure it's not just a couple of horny teenagers?" asked another.

"Look at them, Mel. They match the description of that couple killed a couple of weeks ago."

"But they're not dead," said one of the women.

"No shit. That's undead right there, Charlotte. Take a good look. If we don't put them down, you could be standing right there with them tomorrow night."

"They've got us surrounded." Devon pulled her against him.

Stella could hear the tightness in his voice, the need to do something loud and clear. Her blood was coursing, her new fangs begging for a larger meal than the rabbits they'd drained earlier.

"Get your stakes ready. The heart, remember that's your only target. Work in teams. Don't let them get you alone," instructed a terse whisper from the woods.

"I don't want this," Devon growled. "We're not the monsters."

Red tinged Stella's view. Her blood sang. She'd never felt so alive. "No, but maybe we need to be. Just this once. They're going to kill us, Dev. I'm not ready for that yet. You and me forever, right?"

He let go of her, meeting her gaze, searching. "Are you sure? I don't know if I can turn this off if I give in. I'm so...hungry."

Stella nodded. "Me too." She licked her lips at the thought of the delicious meal slinking toward them. A feast.

A tiny voice screamed in her head, begging her to run.

This was self-defense. Kill or be killed, she assured her conscience. She hadn't asked for this. She hadn't gone looking for trouble. They'd been good, sticking to animals and staying away from temptation. They'd been happy.

Until now.

Excitement sent electric tingles through her body, energizing her for what was to come.

"We could run," said Devon. "We're faster."

"We're stronger too. Can't you hear it? The blood in their veins?"

He groaned. "Just one meal. This is the only one and then it's back to rabbits. Promise me, Stel."

"Sure, yes. Can we please do this now? I'm so hungry, I can't think."

"Yes." He let out a strangled sigh and then took a deep breath of the night air. His voice deepened and his eyes grew darker. "Let's eat," he announced as if he were presenting her with Thanksgiving dinner.

Before she could move, he was already half way across the playground, speeding toward the trees where the outline of one of their attackers crouched.

She bolted to the next visible body, sinking her fangs into the woman's neck. The woman struggled, crying. Stella held her in place as if she were nothing more than a ragdoll. Blood pumped into her mouth, sliding down her throat like the sweetest honey. She couldn't get enough.

A gun fired. Then another. A bullet sunk into her back. Stella threw the drained woman to the ground and spun to face a man with a gun. Would his blood taste the same? She rushed at him to find out.

"Stakes. Not bullets," shouted one of the men still in the woods.

Sucking down her next magnificent meal, Stella spotted Devon, two more bodies at his feet and a limp third in his grasp. He grinned at her, blood running down his face.

"So much better than rabbits," he said, grabbing his next victim.

Bodies poured out of the trees, two firing guns, the rest brandishing stakes. They barreled toward her and Devon. Bullets knocked her back. They hurt, but more like a sting than what she imagined a gunshot should feel like. Devon dropped to his knees, his legs riddled with bleeding wounds.

She started for him but the men wielding stakes beat her to him. They plunged one into his chest. Devon shrieked, his eyes rolling back into his head, as his body went stiff. Black fissures ran over his suddenly grey skin as though someone had scribbled over his flesh. She stared in horror as he burst into pieces that turned to ash a second later.

There would be no forever.

Stella screamed, her vision flashing red with black spots racing in at the edges. She tore into one body after another, ripping throats open, beyond caring about the blood. Her only thought was to punish them all. She wouldn't make them drink, not like her attackers had. She wasn't like them. These people would simply die.

The last man standing held his stake poised to strike. He lunged for her just as she dove for his neck. The cold, hard stake sunk into her chest. His blood flooded her mouth but she couldn't swallow. In the blood-slicked grass, Stella felt her body come apart.

As the last man went silent, ash swirled upward, blowing in the wind.

FRAY FARM

The open house at Fray Farm was hopping. A crowd of prospective buyers swarmed the realtor. Half of the platter of store-bought cookies had already been consumed and the case of bottled water looked like a mostly deflated balloon. An invisible ghostly audience stood on the stairs, studying the swarm in the kitchen.

Della pointed toward one of the prospective buyers. The young man with black-rimmed glasses, a shaggy haircut, and a well-defined body beneath his skin-tight t-shirt and jeans stood beside the kitchen counter eating a cookie.

"Oh, he looks promising."

Ferdinand rolled his eye and shook what remained of his half-blown-off head. "Seriously, Della. He's more interested in a gym membership than moving furniture or doing yard work."

"Agreed. He's only in town for one of those tech jobs. He'll likely leave it in a few years for something bigger and better," Harvey said.

"What about them?" Della pointed to a couple in their thirties. "They look nice."

Harvey curled his upper lip and gave her the side eye. "We agreed on no kids. Look at them, holding hands and all googly-eyed. She'll be popping one out in nine months flat as soon as they have a place of their own. *This* is not their place."

Ferdinand nodded. "We'll keep looking."

Greg flitted above the crowd and met them on the stairs. "I don't know how long I can hold this realtor off. He wants his commission and he's had three offers today. It's getting harder to control his body. He really wants this sale."

"Maybe you're just not very good at controlling bodies." Della sniffed. She gathered her skirt in one hand and held the railing with the other as she descended the stairs with a crooked, hobbling gait.

"Way to go, Greg," said Harvey. "Now Della is going to make a mess of controlling that man's body. You know she's no good at faking manly mannerisms."

"Hey old man, if you want to take over, be my guest. I bet your ghostly ass can't even beat fair lady Della to the kitchen, let alone work your transparent, over-weight spirit into that realtor's finely-tailored suit."

Harvey glared at the pompous and waifish Gregory Allen Fray. "Maybe you shouldn't have driven me into a depression where all I wanted to do was eat, Greg. Or made Ferdinand think he was crazy so that he blew his head half-off. Or maybe, if you'd let us properly explain the household situation to fair Miss Della, she wouldn't have fainted when she caught a glimpse of love-struck Ferdinand here and fallen down these very stairs. But no. So here we are, the farm falling apart around us because everyone thinks this damned place is haunted."

Greg laughed. "And look, buyers everywhere! I told you haunted houses would be in demand someday. We'll have a new house steward by the end of this showing. You'll see."

"Can we at least agree to chase the next steward off before they die here? No one else needs to be trapped in your haunted heaven," Harvey said.

"Sure, yeah, fine," Greg waved for him to shut up.

The three of them watched anxiously as Della stood beside the realtor until his pitch had come to an end with the young couple. As the two of them wandered off hand in hand to explore the house, Della stepped into the realtor. His body shuddered and then he leaned languidly against the kitchen counter, smiling at the stairs. The realtor winked.

Ferdinand groaned. "No one actually does that. No one. Stand up for heaven's sake, you look like a lounge singer draped over a damned piano."

"She can't hear you," Greg noted. "It's surprisingly loud in the kitchen. All that tile we had Della put in when she was alive, it makes everything echo."

"Maybe she should warn them the place is cursed.

That would get rid of the echo problem. Besides, none of these people will work," Harvey groused.

Greg sniffed. "My farm is not cursed, I'll have you know. It's blessed. I spent everything I made in the war to make the talisman that keeps us alive."

"Alive?" Ferdinand waved his arm through the stairway balusters.

"In a manner of speaking," Greg said, glaring at him. "Everyone who dies here gets to live here forever." He smiled wistfully. "Our own little heaven."

"Maybe for you. None of us agreed to your forever, Greg." Harvey stomped up the stairs. "I'm going to bed. Maybe we'll have better luck at the open house next weekend."

The realtor jerked upright. One eye twitched. Several of the people nearby noticed, giving him odd looks. They mumbled to each other and headed for the front door.

Moments after, everyone left but the couple who was chatting quietly in the library off the sitting room. Della heaved herself out of the realtor. The man stumbled against the counter, flinging the cookies and the newspaper he'd been reading earlier onto the floor.

Della limped back to the stairway. "He's going to talk that couple into buying the farm. He hates this place and wants to be done with it."

"Way to go, Della," said Greg. "I'll make sure they put the babies in your room."

The front door opened. A forty-something

woman in a baggy sweater covered in cat hair walked in. She peered around, nodding slowly as she shifted her bulging purse around on her shoulder. A tall metal water bottle and naked-chested romance book cover shifted in and out of view until she got them settled into place.

Greg whistled. "That's the one."

"Maybe for you," Ferdinand grumbled. "I like my women more refined. And you know she's got at least six cats. I mean, look at all that fur."

"I like cats," said Della. "It would be nice to have another woman to talk to. Eventually, I mean." She headed for the library. "I'll get rid of the other two."

Greg leapt off the stairs, floating down to the floor with practiced ease.

"Showoff," yelled Ferdinand.

Intent on making the transaction happen without any mishaps, Greg strode over to the newcomer as she approached the realtor. He was busy picking up everything that had fallen off the counter.

She leaned down to help him, grabbing the newspaper. Shaking it out to straighten it, she laughed at the headline. "'Vampire Hunt Ends in Brutal Massacre?' Who reads this garbage?" She folded the paper neatly and set it on the counter.

The realtor smiled weakly and then launched into his pitch.

"Five bedrooms? That's perfect. I foster cats." She clapped her hands together. "I can do a room for kittens, elderly cats, special needs... Oh, and a playroom! They'll love me at the shelter. I'll take it."

"Wonderful," said the realtor. He reached into his briefcase to pull out a folder. "Just a little paperwork to make an official offer and you'll be on your way to homeownership."

Greg grinned. While the cat part wasn't ideal, she was bound to get sick of that after a few years. He and the others could help that along by antagonizing the cats if they got to be too troublesome.

The realtor shot up straight and looked around wildly. "What's that smell?"

The woman signed her name on the last paper. She scowled. "Smoke?"

The realtor, the cat-lady, and Greg bolted to the library.

Della stood beside the young woman, both staring wide-eyed at the flames leaping up from the vanilla-scented candle the realtor had lit earlier to cover what he'd called 'musty old book stench'. The delicate floor-to-ceiling drapes had been in the house since Ferdinand's time.

Flames quickly licked over to the shelves lined with brittle old books that hadn't been touched since Greg had died. They leapt to an antique tapestry that had been Harvey's most cherished possession and onward to the stacks of antique piano sheet music that Della had collected, even though there was no piano in the house.

"What did you do?" screamed Greg.

Tears rolled down Della's face. "She really wanted the house and wouldn't leave. I thought I'd try the husband, but when I slipped out of her, she freaked out and knocked the candle into the drapes. I didn't mean to!"

Before the four living souls could get back into the sitting room, the exit was engulfed in flames. Greg watched in horror as fire burned all around him, cracking and snapping, devouring the home he loved. Devouring the people who were trapped in it.

Della fled through the smoke and heat. Greg watched her hobble up the stairs even as fire spilled out of the library. Flames ate the rugs, the original wood flooring, and the antique furniture. The walls covered in layers of paper, the first put up by his grandmother when the farm had been built, were a particular delicacy, consumed in a rabid frenzy by the fire.

Screams filled the air, though black smoke hid what the fire had done to the living beings around him. They coughed and sputtered and fell to the ground.

The glass in the library windows exploded, letting in the chilly fall breeze which further stoked the fire until it became a raging inferno. Greg ran to the wall beside the great stone fireplace in the sitting room. The air there was already thick with smoke. Flames danced around him. Plaster turned black overhead. Fire leapt up the stairs, devouring the worn wood and papered walls.

Someone tapped his shoulder.

Greg spun around.

"What's going on?" asked the blackened ghost of the cat-lady in a raspy voice between coughs.

The shapes of three more burned bodies shambled behind her.

"This wasn't supposed to happen," Greg shrieked.

The wall beside the fireplace bubbled and blistered. The white-painted trim cracked and snapped, blackening.

"No!" He dove to the floor, holding his hands over the trim, trying to press it back into place. His hands pushed right through it, and yet even in doing so, he couldn't grasp the carved wooden talisman hidden behind the board.

The four new ghosts staggered toward the door. None of them could open it, their hands slipping through the knob. They made dreadful moaning noises.

Della screamed from the floor above. Harvey slid down the remnants of the stairs while Ferdinand floated awkwardly behind him with Della in his arms. They joined the others at the door.

Another window shattered. Harvey ran to it, but couldn't make his body flow like the smoke that rolled outside.

Flames ate the trim that had guarded the talisman for a hundred and fifty-three years. Something in the kitchen exploded with a deafening pop. The fire roared.

Tears flowed from Greg's eyes as he watched the fire consume the talisman he'd so carefully hidden.

One by one the new ghosts evaporated.

"I'm not ready!" shrieked Della. "I'm not—"

"Della!" Ferdinand reached for where she'd stood a second ago and then he too was gone.

Harvey cast Greg a mournful look. "On to the real heaven this time."

The large man's transparent body sputtered and then where he stood were only flames.

Greg sighed, looking at the farm that had been in his family for generations, the one thing he'd sworn to care for and had done so even into death. Another hour and it would be no longer.

A tremor ran through his body, a vibration that built until he couldn't move or even think. The air around him was suddenly an inferno. An inferno he could feel. His skin blistered. The stench of burning hair flooded his mouth and nose. Greg screamed. This was nothing like the first time when he'd died peacefully in his sleep in the upstairs bedroom. This was horrible and painful and it didn't end.

The ruins of Fray farm smoked for days. Those that came to search for remains swore they could hear faint screaming, but the logical ones among them knew it was probably just the wind.

THE SESSION

Andreas checked the clock on his office wall. Five minutes until his next appointment. He spent one minute jotting notes in Mr. Danbury's file about his fascination with haunted houses. Three more went to meditating so Andreas could keep his cravings under control. The last one was taken up with doing a little glamour touch-up on his appearance. It wouldn't do to make a bad impression on his newest client. After all, therapist sessions paid the bills quite nicely, not to mention the other benefits.

He heard the outer office door open. Sandra, his receptionist, greeted the new client. Minutes stretched out as papers shuffled on Sandra's desk. New intake paperwork. Andreas shuddered. Thank goodness he had Sandra to deal with all the official trappings of his profession.

When the new client did finally open the door and peek his head inside, Andreas smiled.

"Welcome, William. Have a seat." He waved to the plush beige chair across from the matching one where he sat.

William, wearing a burgundy cardigan, grey slacks, a pressed white shirt, and black slip-on shoes settled into the chair. He folded his hands on his lap and gazed steadily at Andreas.

Sandra slipped in, handing Andreas a clipboard with the one standard form that provided the pertinent information he needed. He glanced over it while asking, "So what brings you here today?"

"I'm having trouble sleeping at night. So much on my mind, you know? So much going on in the world today that is just out of control. Out of *my* control, I mean."

Andreas nodded. Another control freak. He sighed inwardly and launched into his usual raft of control-related questions. At the forty-five-minute mark, he leaned forward, tapping his pen rhythmically on the clipboard.

"I'm glad you came to me. I feel this is something I can help you with. It may take a few sessions, but I think that as long as you're willing to do the work, you'll be on your way to restful nights very soon."

William smiled. "You came well recommended. Everyone says you're the best at solving issues quickly rather than milking clients for years of session fees."

"I do my best to help." Andreas slowed the pen tapping until he could hear William's heart matching the same beat. He perched on the edge of his chair, locking onto William's gaze. "When you feel out of control, you will breathe in slowly and relax. Repeat what I said."

"Breathe slowly and relax," William said in a distant voice.

"Wake now."

William blinked, glancing around the room as though he'd just missed something. "Is our time up?"

"I'll see you next week. See Sandra for scheduling on your way out."

Once the door closed and William's footsteps left Sandra's desk, Andreas stood and walked to the mini fridge under the cabinet behind his desk. Opening the door, he perused the available meals inside. His mouth watered when he spotted the vial labeled Tara Jacobs. The little girl's blood had the most delectable flavor. Perhaps, due to her age, he could convince her mother to bring her for a few more sessions before he cut her lose. He didn't keep any of his clients too long. No need to be greedy when it was so easy to get free meals.

As he savored the sweetness of Tara Jacobs, taking sips from the vial to make her last as long as possible, he wondered what William would taste like. The first session was always a freebie. Next week, he'd pay like all the others.

Wednesday afternoon rolled around, again bringing William to sit across from Andreas. They talked about William's hour-long commute, his boss that didn't respect him, and his wife that liked to shop whether they could afford it or not. All in all, it was pretty standard. Andreas got to the forty-five-minute mark and leaned forward to begin his pen tapping. Once he had William in thrall, he suggested listening to audiobooks to make the drive more relaxing, working out a budget with his wife, and that William be more assertive with his boss. Once business was taken care of, Andreas nicked a vein in William's neck with his razor-sharp fingernail and filled a clean vial. After labeling it with William's name and the date, he stored it in the fridge, washed his hands, and resumed his position in his chair.

"Wake," he commanded.

William smiled. "Thank you. That was very helpful. I understand completely now why I've been feeling so out of control."

Already thinking of which vial he would drink at the end of the day, Andreas nodded absently and set the clipboard with his few notes jotted for William's file on his desktop. "Wonderful. I look forward to seeing you next week."

Instead of leaving, William stood in front of Andreas. "I don't think so."

Andreas glanced up at the sudden appearance of

the man invading his space. He felt his glamour flicker as anger rushed to the surface of his manufactured demeanor.

"Is there a problem, William?"

"Yes."

Shadows grew in the room, the light seeming to be sucked into the man in front of him. William grew taller, straighter, and an inhuman blackness flooded his eyes.

"You were given a gift and this is what you do with it? You eat meager tidbits from the fodder? You *help* them? Ridiculous. And embarrassment."

William called out, a heavy compulsion in the voice that mimicked Andreas, "Sandra, could you come in here?"

"Don't hurt her," Andreas ground out. "She's vital to my practice."

"You no longer have a practice. Not in my town."

William's fingers shifted into talons as they ripped into the flesh of Andreas's chest, exposing his heart. Andreas scrambled to hold the withered organ in place, to summon the strength to heal himself. The strict diet he'd been on since his transformation thirty-one years ago may have made it easy to blend in with the humans, but it kept his vampire abilities at a minimum. He'd never required full strength before.

Sandra walked in, all sensible heels, office casual, and a neat ponytail peppered with greys that hadn't been there when he'd first hired her. "Did you need—"

"Run!" Andreas shouted.

William was faster, already on her before Sandra had a chance to turn back to the door. Andreas couldn't watch. The sounds of the wet rending of flesh, of chewing, slurping... He darted to the refrigerator and began pouring vials of blood down his throat, swallowing as though he had an insatiable thirst.

Life rushed through his veins, power, strength. His vision sharpened, the room taking on finer details and colors he hadn't seen since his first days as a vampire when he was learning how to control the demon inside. Control didn't matter, only living to see another day. He healed the deep gash in his chest with a thought.

Andreas roared, his fangs at full length, his body pumped full of last week's appointments. "How dare you come into my office and attack me?"

William dropped Sandra's glistening, fleshless torso onto the blood-soaked carpet. "How dare I? How dare you taunt the fodder to discover us with every day of your pathetic existence? Their numbers are many and we are few. If they were to discover the truth, they could overpower us. I am not ready to die just so you can help the fodder sleep better at night."

"No one suspected. No one knew." Andreas pointed to Sandra's mutilated corpse. "That is the kind of evidence that will get us discovered!"

William rushed at Andreas, talons at the ready, fangs covered in Sandra's blood. "I suspected. You aren't as clever as you think you are. Only evening hours. An eerily impressive high client rating online. No complaints. Everyone neatly compliant. It reeked of compulsion."

He swiped again but this time Andreas had his vampire speed. William's foot rolled over the top of one of the discarded vials. He stumbled. Andreas leapt on him, tearing into the undead flesh with his own razor talons.

"You invade my office." He bit into William's neck, carving out a mouthful of flesh. He spit the vile mass of decay onto the floor. Bright red blood gushed from the wound.

"You kill my assistant." He held William down with one hand and drove his other into William's chest, seeking out his heart. When he had it, he yanked it out and shoved it in William's now pale face.

"You ruin my life here." He shook his head. "Now I will end yours."

Andreas threw the beating heart onto the floor and ground it into the carpet with the heel of his shoe. William writhed and shrieked, growing weaker with each second that he was parted from the key to the demon that animated them.

When Andreas was confident that William couldn't rise, he dropped the vampire and threw the remains of the crushed organ into his trashcan. A quick search of his desk yielded a lighter. The paper in his trash caught easily. The demon-infused heart sputtered a moment, but then accepted the flame.

William went silent. As quickly as his heart was consumed by fire, so did his body turn to ash.

The fire activated the sprinkler system. Water poured down on the chaos of his office, making the ink run on the vials and washing the blood and ash deep into the carpet.

Andreas surveyed the devastation William had caused. His gaze landed on Sandra and the certificate on the wall that he'd used to help people. He would move, start over, and find a new Sandra. But having tasted his full power, he wouldn't collect vials. William was right about that diet being pathetic. He could control the urges. Andreas ran his tongue over his fangs. He could.

BLUE WARNING

I shifted my tentacles yet again, trying to find room under the long table surrounded by bipeds. Just when I'd found safe havens for all six of my appendages, the door at the end of the room opened and everyone stood. I slid over the edge of my seat and followed suit.

A man in a green uniform said, "Mr. President, thank you for joining us."

Finally, after three days of interrogation and examinations, these creatures were giving me the meeting I'd asked for. I faced the human with silver hair and sagging skin. "Mr. President, you need to evacuate."

The uniformed man held up his hand. "Hold on there, Blue. Let the man have a seat."

"That's not my..." My eye stalk sagged. I'd attempted to convey the pronunciation of my name countless times but they couldn't seem to grasp it. I let it go and concentrated on trying to get them to understand the gravity of my message. "You are all in grave danger."

The bipeds poured water into glasses. They paged through folders adorned with official-looking seals. Several of the suit-wearing individuals whispered to one another while casting glances in my direction.

I took a deep breath of the oxygen-heavy air and double-checked my translator. Their high-pitched noise seemed clear enough to me and the output light was lit. I tried speaking slower and louder. "You need to evacuate. The Neitnoids have been devouring planets in galaxies near yours. You don't have much time."

The president leaned toward a younger male next to him. "Did the blue thing just say something is devouring planets, Jim?"

"He did, sir."

I wanted to wrap a tentacle around one of their thin necks and shake some sense into them, but that went against the rules listed in my job guidelines. Besides, I'd always suspected that my boss gave me the most aggravating assignments in the hopes that I'd quit. He'd never liked the lengthy and thorough mission reports that I prided myself on, but I wasn't about to miss out on a promotion just because he didn't like paperwork.

"General?" The president jutted his chin at a white-haired man.

The metals on the general's uniform jingled as he stood to face me. "Let's start at the top, shall we? Who do you work for?"

"The safety division of the UPWS, Universal Planetary Well-being Services."

"Do you plan on coming to our rescue? I mean, is this some ploy to get us to submit to your people in return for protection?"

"Nothing like that. I'm only here to warn you."

A pointy foot covering met with the sensitive tip of one of my tentacles. I yelped and wound my throbbing appendage around the base of the hard, square chair that barely contained my rotund bulk.

The other males and females muttered to one another, sending my translator into a frenzy as it tried to decipher everything at once.

"So this UPWS, they run the universe or something?" The general chuckled. "We didn't sign up for that."

I'd been over all of this with men in white robes while spending the last few days in their decontamination chamber. It had seemed like they'd understood me well enough. Maybe they'd not clearly conveyed my message to their superiors. "In light of the Neitnoid threat, representatives have been dispatched to all habitable planets in their range."

Habitable was a negotiable term after seeing what these creatures had done to theirs. Perhaps it would be in the best interest of the other planets throughout the universe if the Neitnoids ate this one. They might get some sort of deadly infection or, at the very least, horrible indigestion.

The president looked around the table. "Do we have anything on file for this UPWS?"

Jim pulled a paper from his folder and slid it to the president. "It's all right here."

Those days I'd spent answering questions had been useful after all. He'd just not had time to read over the information I'd given them.

"Ah, yes," said the president. "Sorry for all the confusion. We don't get alien visitors every day."

I didn't need his apologies, I needed assurance that this last planet on my list had received and understood my message so I could head home.

"You're not safe. There is a very real threat out there." I jabbed a tentacle toward the sky. "By my calculations, you only have a couple of weeks."

"A couple of week's warning isn't much of a heads up," said the president. "You show up here all gloom and doom and don't offer a single ray of hope?"

"The Extermination Division of the UPWS is working on eliminating the danger. However, they have several threats sapping their limited resources. I wouldn't rely solely on them to protect you."

"You hear that, Mr. President? Blue says we should protect ourselves."

"Get the Air Force on it."

My portable database offered little on their military resources other than it was inadequate—certainly so for the level of threat the Neitnoids presented. "That won't do any good. You need to evacuate."

The general glared at me. "No good? What do you know about our Air Force, you tentacled, blue, cyclops-looking freak? Nothing. That's right. Nothing. Why don't you just fly back to your friends and tell them to leave us alone, or we'll show them what good we can do." He nodded to the president and left the room.

Maybe his absence would make the rest of them more willing to listen to reason. "The Neitnoids are not my friends. They will not listen to me or anyone else. You need to leave. Get to one of your other colonies and gather your forces until the Extermination Division can assist you."

The remaining humans muttered to one another. One of them cleared his throat. "We don't have other colonies."

I checked my records. Sure enough, no other known colonies, no known mass space travel abilities, and no military force advanced enough to ward off the threat. Previous scouting reports had estimated that they'd have been developed beyond this point several cycles ago.

Unless the Neitnoids changed course, got full, or the Extermination Division swooped in to save the day, this world was doomed. "Well, you have your Air Force. I'm sure you'll be fine."

The president heaved a relieved sigh. "Good.

Good. Thank you for the warning." He sat back and smiled. "I hope you don't have to rush off. We'd love to have you stay a while and tell us all about the other planets you've visited. We find that sort of thing fascinating."

"I have a long journey home ahead of me. I should go." And I had a lot of files to update and reports to write. I couldn't bear the thought of another UPWS employee sent here as misinformed about their advancement and hospitality as I had been.

"I'm afraid we can't let you leave just yet. Your ship's landing caused us enough trouble. The idea of aliens on our planet would cause our people to panic. We'll have to arrange a special time for your departure to keep order amongst the masses."

The president tapped Jim's shoulder. "Why don't you give our guest a tour of our visitor facility in the desert so he can be more comfortable?"

A day to relax in comfort sounded wonderful after all the aggravation these creatures had put me through. Maybe they weren't so bad after all. "Would you like a ride in my ship, Jim?"

Jim rose. "I'm afraid we can't take your ship. It's already at the facility, waiting for you. How about a limo ride? I bet you've never had one of those."

Land transports seemed so primitive, but from what I'd found, the limo was one of their highest-ranking social forms. He was giving me an honor. "That sounds nice."

The president and the others filed out the same door that the general had used. Jim went to the one on the other side of the room where I'd entered.

"Follow me." Jim led me down the hallway, past the decontamination room, and through a door that brought us outside. A dark sky greeted me with twinkling stars. Soon I'd be back among them, speeding homeward.

Men folded in and out of the surrounding darkness, opening doors to the waiting limo and directing narrow beams of light to guide the way.

The long limo and lack of any feet other than Jim's offered me plenty of room to stretch out. The seat was still the wrong shape, and I struggled to find a suitable way to recline in it.

Darkened windows offered little view of the scenery and divided us from the driver. Jim filled the hours by asking questions about my job, my homeworld, and the planets I'd visited.

We stopped at one point and the front window rolled down enough for a brown bag to be shoved through. Jim grabbed it and shuffled through what sounded like crinkly paper inside. When he pulled his hand from the bag, he held a stinky, steaming round object that he thrust into his mouth. He chewed for a moment.

"Sorry, we don't have anything suitable for you to eat right now. The visitor facility will have a feast waiting for you."

A feast, a real bed, a few hours of silence, it all sounded so good. I bobbed my eye stalk and waited for the ride to be over.

I'd almost drifted off to sleep when the limo stopped. Jim had developed dark circles under his eyes. The bag that had contained his earlier meal smelled even worse than it had before. The second the door opened, I spilled out to find myself surrounded by searing, dry heat.

"Right this way." Jim held out his hand as if to gracefully reveal the mammoth metal building in front of me. Uniformed humans stood beside an open door. They avoided looking at us as we went inside.

Once my vision adjusted to the less blaring light, I spotted my ship. Then I saw several others of various models sitting near it. They might not have visitors often, but they did have them. I wondered if they'd all been treated as rudely as I had. "How long have the others been waiting for their clearance to leave?"

Jim glanced over his shoulder. "I'm not sure. That's not my department."

"I hope it won't be too long. Your planet might be the last stop for this mission, but I have a job to get back to and reports to file."

I imagined my boss's face when I handed him my filled data crystal and laughed. He couldn't fire me, my record was spotless. Surely, he'd promote me so we wouldn't have to work together any longer. That was the only solution to making us both happy once and for all.

"Don't worry. I'll check into a departure time for you," said Jim.

"Thank you." I knew where my ship was now. Leaving on my own schedule would be rude but certainly possible. This world was about to be eaten. Panic among the occupants wouldn't make much of a difference. I considered leaving right then, but a meal and sleep before the journey were too tempting to pass up.

An elevator took us down two levels. Cool air flowed through the metal doors as they slid open to reveal a circular room lined with more doors. Two armed men stood on either side of the elevator. Jim ignored them and they ignored us.

"Here we are. I believe room three has a vacant bed." Jim slid a card through a reader and entered a code on a wall pad next to the door marked with a black number three. He held the door open as I passed him. "Enjoy."

I stepped into a long, dimly lit space.

The door closed. A lock clicked, echoing a metallic thunk through the room.

I twisted around to discover he'd not followed me inside. "Jim?"

"He can't hear you through the door," said a voice from the shadows. "What line did they get you with?"

My eye stalk extended, searching for the source of the voice. "What do you mean? I'm waiting for my departure clearance."

A naked, bulbous-headed, grey alien stepped into the light. "I've been waiting for six cycles."

I gasped. "But our ships are right up there. Why not just leave?"

He bowed. "It's nice to see someone new. My previous roommate died a cycle ago." Bones showed through his skin and a glassy film covered his big, black eyes. "They don't let us out of the room. They're fascinated with us. Always filling little vials with blood or any other fluid they can get out of you. And the questions," he groaned, "they never end."

Trapped? I draped myself over one of the beds. Human beds were not at all what I'd been hoping for. "But I answered all their questions, many of them repeatedly."

He drifted over to my side and patted one of my tentacles. "What were you doing here?"

"UPWS Safety Department. I'm delivering a planetary threat warning. You?"

"Extermination Department, scouting wave." He reached under the mattress I was sitting on and pulled out a silver device.

I reached out to touch it.

"You don't want to do that. Even their probes couldn't find where I had this hidden."

I cringed and clenched my tentacles together, remembering my own probing.

He cradled the object in his hands as if it were

his most precious possession. "It's the one thing I was able to get off my ship. My timer. Just twelve more hours until it's all over."

"That's wonderful news. The humans will let us go when our forces save them." Hope swelled within me. I'd live to see my promotion after all. "I didn't realize we were so close to exterminating the Neitnoids."

"I wasn't here for the Neitnoids." His lipless mouth curled into a smile and he pointed to the door. "We're eliminating *them*."

JUSTICE

Thousands stood in the rain. Women, men, and children, they all cowered outside the walls without anything to protect them. The king had ordered their deaths and it was my job to see the decree carried out. Not looking made it easier.

Drops pelted down on the stone roof overhead. Safe beneath it, my men turned the heavy wheels that closed the gate. A loud clank reverberated through the air.

"It's a horrible death," whispered Colin, who stood beside me.

I nodded, not wanting to give words to what I knew to be happening out there. This wasn't the first time I'd carried out this sentence, but the Thorens were honorable folk. They didn't deserve this.

They remained stoic as thunder rumbled across the sky. Rain poured down.

Even the youngest among them kept silent longer than I imagined I could have if my skin were being eaten away by drops of acid. Drop by drop. Screams filled the air. I longed to cover my ears, but it would mark me a coward in front of my men. I was to listen, to report back the terror and suffering to the king, to delight him with the tales of his justice.

Colin peered out at the dark clouds. "How long do you think this one will last?"

"Long enough. Get away from the roofline. You want to get burned?" The younger man was a good aide, but he was prone to clumsiness.

"No one wants to get burned," Colin said.

"Of course not. The best way to avoid it is to—"

"Not anger the king?"

"Quiet." I glanced around, making sure no one was in earshot. "You want to end up out there?"

Colin blinked slowly, head cocked. "No?"

"Then shut up. Get me some tea."

"Tea, sir?"

"Was I speaking in another language?"

"I don't know any other languages."

"Exactly." I pointed to the doorway behind us. "Go."

The rest of my men stood inside their stone towers along the wall, watching. I would have sent them all inside if I could have gotten away with it. With each rain sentence, the men grew a little colder, the lines on their faces, deeper. They ate less, cared less, and drank more.

I tried to concentrate on the paperwork before

me, but the screams made it hard. By the time Colin returned with a steaming cup in his hand, their volume had decreased by more than half. People were dead out there, usually the parents. The children, shielded by other bodies were often the last to die.

Those we left outside ceased to be people. We'd only find bumpy bits of bone, metal, and sometimes scraps of boiled leather once the storm had passed.

As I sipped my tea, I silently prayed for the clouds to part and the sun to shine so that some might remain alive, that my king might find enough decency to offer pardons. The gods answered with lightning that arced along the clouds. Rain poured down harder. I threw my cup against the stone wall, watching it shatter into tiny white shards. It wasn't the thing I truly wished to smash, but it sufficed for a moment.

"Sir?"

"It was cold. Get me something to eat."

Colin sputtered. "The tea was hot. I saw to it myself."

"Just go get me something to eat."

He backed away, watching me with wide eyes.

I waved him off and stared at the papers. The predictors said we wouldn't have another rain for months. The dry season was almost upon us. My heart swelled at the thought.

But the king would grow sullen. He liked the attention, the futile attacks of the other tribes who sought the safety of our home.

The rain ate so much. Most had to huddle underground in caves or take their chances in the old places. As far as we knew, we were the only safe ones. The lucky. The rain did not have a taste for our stone.

Deep under the fortress, an intricate web of tunnels sheltered those who did not wish to dwell within the walls above ground. Our food grew there, under the safety of lights from the generators, beside where the fresh water flowed. If I was lucky, Colin would travel all the way there and back before returning.

The Thorens were among the larger tribes. Even then, they had failed to penetrate our walls. The Chitans, Gelmesh, and Itods stood out amongst the others eliminated during my years of service. How many others had survived the angry skies and still roamed out there in the wastes? How many others would our selfish king refuse to shelter?

We had room. Plenty of it, and the means to make more if needed. Barrels of fuel for the earth movers sat safely in a cavern far below, guarded day and night. I assigned my men there as long as I could, rotating through them, but the downtime wasn't helping them maintain their morality as much as it used to.

Outside, the screaming stopped, though the rain continued. There was nothing I could do here. It was time to report to the king. Colin would find me eventually.

I shuffled the papers together, shoved them in

my satchel, and left it on the table. He'd take care of that too.

The walk down from the walls was a long one, bound up in winding stairways that provided safety from the rain. Round and round and downward I went until I finally came to the bottom. Men nodded and saluted as I passed by. I straightened my uniform before entering the main fortress. The king's guard were picky about that sort of thing. Always looking immaculate as they were, I rather doubted any of them had ever seen a true day of labor in the tunnels. They were his friends, promoted when he took the throne from his father back when I was just a young man.

The first pair of guards stood outside the hall. Their thin arms and skinny necks protruded from their crisp white leather vests. Silken shirts covered what the vest did not. Their uniforms shone in the light of the humming bulbs above. Heavy clubs hung from their belts, painted white to match the rest. The paint bore not a single scratch. I'd never seen them used. Mine was dented, old, oiled, and well-worn. Cherished. A symbol of my rank. There hadn't been any new timber in generations. There must have been trees somewhere, but we'd not seen any and no one came looking to trade them.

The guards opened the door for me and stepped aside. The king was waiting.

He sat on his throne in his fur-edged robe. It was an archaic thing, but as in so many other matters, he hadn't asked my opinion. The red velvet padding on the chair highlighted his pale skin. Grey flecked his neatly-trimmed beard. The room stunk of the cloying incense he insisted be lit in his presence. I preferred the smell of moist underground air and damp stone to his stench.

"The prisoners?"

"Dead, your grace."

He rubbed his hands together. "A well-deserved end."

"They only sought shelter."

"They attacked." He looked me up and down, evaluating, judging.

My skin crawled. "Yes, they did." But they hadn't. They'd asked for shelter. They'd begged, pleaded, and pounded their fists on our walls. That had been the extent of their assault, fists on stone. Other tribes had made feeble attacks, but even thousands strong, the Thorens used no weapons. They'd not laid out any attempt at a siege. They hadn't even tried to infiltrate with spies or agents. They'd asked and been denied and then sentenced to death, every last one.

"Tell me. Tell me how they suffered."

"We marched the fools through the fortress they'd sought to take from us, made them see all we had despite their efforts."

The king nodded his approval. "Which gate?"

"We opened the south gate and forced them back outside the walls as the clouds gathered. As predicted, the rain came. The gate was closed. They screamed, all of them, long and loud until the rain had exacted their punishment." The words were sour on my tongue.

"And the children? You checked for any living?"

"There were no survivors." There never were.

His thick lips stretched into a grin. "Good. This is our home and we will share it with no one. Soon they will all learn."

"Soon they will all be dead," I said.

The four men who flanked the king looked bored. They'd heard these reports before. They were supposed to act as his council, but they all did whatever he wanted. Just like the rest of us. Just like me. I'd just killed an entire unarmed tribe of people because he told me to. I hated this man. Even more, I hated myself.

"Yes," said the king. "They will all die."

And then we'd be alone with the blood-thirsty king. What would make him smile then?

My conscience couldn't bear any more lives extinguished for his amusement.

My hand slipped to the club at my side. I could save the lives of anyone who might still come to us for shelter.

Colin, my men, I could offer them ease. I could save us all.

I could kill the king.

Muscles tensed, I took note of the four guards and sprang forward. The club swung free of the strap in a fluid motion, arching upward with my arm. The floor sped beneath my feet as I bounded up the stairs to the throne and the gaping man sitting upon it. Wood crashed against his skull with a wet thud and a crack. The king fell sideways, spilling out of his chair and rolling down the steps. Blood, brain, and bits of bone trailed behind him.

His mouth hung open but never would another order be uttered from it. I'd killed him. The king was dead. We were all free.

"He killed the king! Seize him."

The guards snapped into motion, seconds too late. Their clubs smacked into my shoulders, knocking me down but doing no serious harm. They weren't strong enough for that. I laughed at them.

One hit me on the back of the head. The room spun. I fell to my knees.

"Is it still raining?" someone asked.

"The king would like that," said one of the others.

They bound my hands behind my back and hauled me to my feet. The six of them led me outside. We stayed under the covered walkways until reaching the main courtyard. One of them blew a horn. Another cried out, "Behold the man who has killed the king."

Pride surged through my veins until they shoved me out from the protection of the roof into the torrents of rain. I staggered several steps before regaining my balance.

Men cried out from up on the walls. My men.

Whether they were cheering for or against me I couldn't tell.

The sting struck me first, pelting my exposed skin like tiny needles. My muscles seized. I couldn't move. Rain soaked into my hair and clothes, warming, and then building up to a burn that took my breath away.

Rocks rained down from above. Not one of them hit me. They bounced off the roof where the six guards stood in their clean, dry white uniforms. Well-aimed rocks hit the men directly from the opposite end of the courtyard. My men were masters of the slingshot.

I caught a glimpse of Colin's sorrow-filled face as he peered down from above. I yelled at him to get back, to get out of the rain. Then my vision blurred. My throat burned. Everything was on fire. I screamed.

Footsteps scuffled on the flagstones. Then there were men beside me. Men in white. Their screams joined mine. I prayed they were the last screams my people would ever hear.

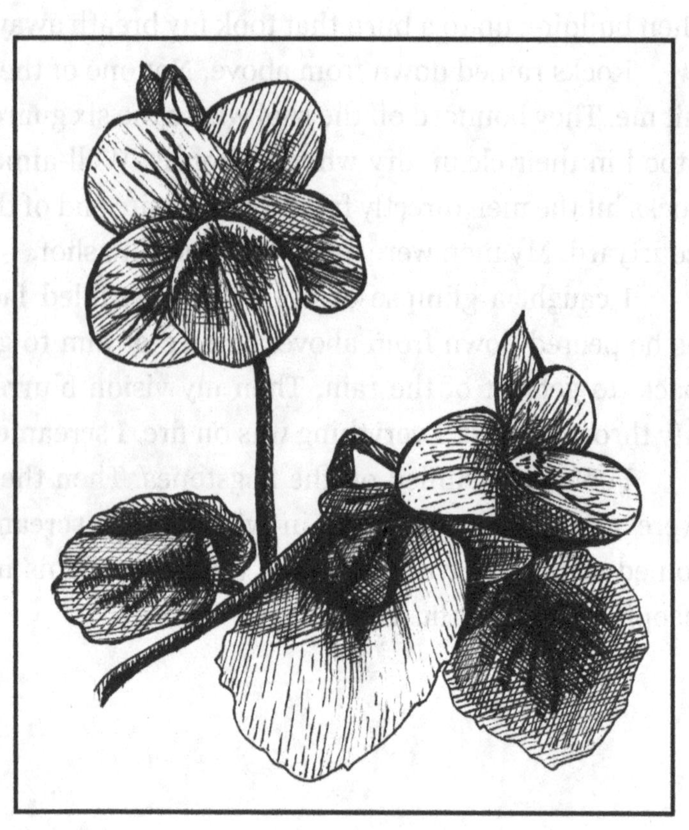

VIOLETS

An afternoon of daydreaming amongst the wildflowers seemed the perfect way to forget about Kevin Valentine. The violets were blooming, both purple and white, which were her favorite. Sitting on a thick rock, worn smooth by thousands of years of rain, she leaned down to plunge her fingers into the thick carpet of heart-shaped leaves. Vanessa was reminded of the pain lodged deep in her chest.

She crumpled the delicate stems and threw the flowers to the ground. He thought he could sweet-talk her into giving him what he wanted and then toss her aside? He had no idea who he was crossing.

Vanessa raised her face to the sky, gathering the summons to the winds. She rested a single finger on the vein on her neck, timing her words with the beat of her heart. Once the spell had been cast, she shed her school uniform. The rumpled pile of cloth mocked her and the life she'd so desperately wanted to have, the one she'd begged her father for. Now, because of

Kevin, of one night, that path had ended.

Already she could feel her father's begrudging gift of a human guise falling away, the soft, brown skin of her hands returning to their usual rough textured grey-brown, flecked with moss. Leaves sprouted in her long hair as it whipped around her face in the rising wind. Her cousins at the edge of the field swayed, murmuring of her return.

Soon her father would hear, and he would toss her failure in her face. Her unconventional proposal of leading her people as a human protector of the forest instead of in her true form had been full of dreams and good intentions. But being human had overshadowed everything, all the emotions, the sensations, they were overwhelming. She'd lost sight of her future for one night with Kevin.

She'd failed and now the task of protector would fall to her brothers.

But where one path ended, another began. She cast a glance at the uniform, cursing her temper, and even more, the boy who had given it cause to flare.

The sky grew closer with each moment of the transformation. Vanessa took a step toward her cousins, her long legs carrying her over a quarter of the meadow in that one motion. But then she reconsidered. If she remained alone, her father wouldn't be able to speak to her. No gloating from him or her brothers, just the winds and the birds. Perhaps children would play in her shade and swing from the lowest of her branches.

Vanessa reached the middle of the meadow just as the roots spiraled from her toes, sinking deep into the fertile soil. Her neck grew thick and strong to support each strand of hair as it sprouted toward the sky.

And then the winds brought Kevin.

He spilled from the dark funnel to roll to a stop in the field of flowers, his eyes wild and feet scrambling to get beneath him. He grabbed her legs to pull himself upright. Blood ran from a gash over one eye and he held one arm to his chest, cradling it with the other. The winds hadn't been gentle with him.

She didn't plan to be either. He'd said he loved her, that they would be together, and she'd given him everything. Now he would give her everything.

Vanessa curled her long fingers around his chest and lifted him from the ground. He screamed, feet kicking madly. His fingers bled as he tried to pry hers away.

"You don't like me now? Am I not pretty enough for you?"

She held him tight as her legs fused, thrusting her higher. Her hips spread becoming a thick trunk. Already the sunlight had faded beneath her canopy. Her mother had made her well.

Kevin writhed and blubbered nonsense. Her human form had found his strong jaw and wide shoulders attractive. His dark eyes had held all manner of promises that night they'd shared together. And so had his lips. Vanessa shuddered, remembering the sensations of their bodies joining together.

Their joining now wasn't quite as magical as she stuffed him in her mouth and swallowed him down, but it was just as fulfilling. She could feel him deep inside, squirming, and beating on her insides with his fists. Soon enough he would accept that they would always be together.

Vanessa let out one last deep sigh, releasing the air that had held open the pocket for Kevin. He went still as the space compressed, filling her with his body until she felt complete.

Her mouth and eyes sealed shut as the last vestiges of her human form dissipated. Vanessa stood alone, a glorious tree in the middle of a meadow flecked with violets. Deep inside her, a lone man screamed.

THE OTHER SIDE OF THE COIN
A NARVAN STORY

We all gathered around the sanctuary were the goddess lay in her splendid tube of light. Surrounded by white and violet flowers, she'd lain silent for months.

When she'd first come to us, she'd been vibrant and powerful. The priest assured us that she still lived, but we'd seen no sign of it. Those that were chosen to touch her tube said that they could feel her power, that she healed them.

We, the children, were not given that honor.

The priest said we weren't ready. Our bodies weren't formed enough to withstand her touch. We were young and whole and didn't need healing. It didn't seem fair that we were only to serve while everyone else listened to the priest's teachings and the chosen got to be in her divine presence.

At eight, I was among the oldest of the useful children. There were too many under five to be help and a few closer to twelve that spend their time ordering us around. Some of us took care of the littles on the below-ground level. They would someday serve the rest of us when we were old enough to join in worshiping of the goddess.

I carried my basket of bread, baked under the supervision of the older children who knew how. Others carried fruit we collected from a storehouse that one of the nine's parents had owned. They'd given him their access code when they'd joined the worshippers. The storehouse was nearly empty now. Though we were sure there were more, we didn't know where they were or how to get into them. We were going to have to figure out something soon or we were all going to starve. The sleeping goddess couldn't save us from that.

Adults stood around me, gazing at the balcony above where the priest had called for the goddess's lighted tube to be displayed. He called for the chosen to come forward. I handed bread to anyone that would accept it. Most of the adults were too busy watching the ceremony to pay attention to what I put in their hands. They were getting so thin, their skin like the crust of the bread in my hand. Every day there seemed to be a few less of them.

One of the twelves had said that from the upper floor, they could see over the wall of the mansion all the way down the hill in front of the towering house. They claimed that there was a stack of bodies in the park on the other side of the street and that people were going there to die. They wouldn't let any of the rest of us look.

I searched for my mother and father, as I did every day, and found them sitting on a thick, low branch in one of the trees near the back of the yard. They sat side by side, holding hands, so busy watching the ceremony that they didn't notice me. They hadn't in weeks.

As I circled back toward the house, my basket empty, I passed by the hill of credit chips, jewels, and trade coins from worlds I'd never heard of. In the early days, the priest had asked for offerings for the goddess, but they sat here just as they had since they'd been left. And even with all of the riches sitting here, she slept, no longer smiling upon us.

What had we done wrong?

"Ern, look." Amilina, one of the nines, pointed to the top of the hill that the mansion was built into. A giant man stood atop the hill, hunched over as though that somehow would make him smaller to all of us below. He gazed over the worshippers, his mouth moving as though he were counting their number. Unaware of the invader, the priest's voice rose as he began a prayer.

The man's head snapped to the balcony and our goddess. Even with the chosen standing around her, the light shone from within, so all knew she was still among us.

Two other people, a woman and a younger copy of the giant man popped up beside him.

"They're here for the goddess," Amilina whispered.

The long coat the man wore parted, revealing weapons strapped to his body. I'd seen men like that who traveled on the ships to the port to deliver goods. My father called them mercs, said their goods were just as likely stolen as legal. He wouldn't do business with them, but others did.

All three of them looked to our goddess as though they too knew what a treasure she was. Maybe they'd met her before on another world.

Amilina huddled close to me, her empty basket in her hands. "Do you think they've come to worship?"

"No. Not men like that. Steal her, more likely."

"The priest won't let them," Amilina decreed.

While none of us dared cross the priest, he had the ear of the goddess after all, that man didn't look like the praying sort. With weapons like he carried, he could kill the priest before the priest even knew he was there.

"Hurry, Amilina." I pointed at the balcony. "Warn him."

She nodded, dropping her basket, and running toward the ground-level door. It would take her several minutes to make it back into the house and up the three flights of stairs to the balcony level.

I ran to the nearest of the other children, warning him of the intruders. He nodded and ran to another as did I. Soon the yard was abuzz with the news. We tried to tell the adults, each of us tugging on arms, on clothes, pinching, holding hands, but nothing we did tore their attention from the blessings the goddess was bestowing on the chosen up on the balcony. The adults around us murmured their prayers, chanting softly for forgiveness, for her blessing.

The man on the hilltop stood tall now, his hands in fists at his sides. The woman and the younger man were out of sight. I sent two of the children inside to warn the others in case the intruders were heading into the house.

"Tell the twelves first! Hurry!" I hoped the twelves would know what to do.

We didn't have weapons in the house. The goddess had banned them. There were knives in the kitchen, but what good were those against a man bigger than six of us together?

He leapt from the top of the hill onto the balcony as if it were no trouble to span the gap as long as he was tall. He landed with a loud clamor. The children on the balcony scattered. The chosen clung to the tube. The priest prayed on. I yelled as loud as I could but I don't think he heard me.

Not knowing what else to do, I hurried to where my parents sat in the tree and climbed up the trunk to wedge myself next to them. They shifted aside as I settled in but it was like they were half-asleep, there, but not really there. All the while, they chanted their prayer. Hoping the goddess would help us, I joined them.

The giant man stood on the balcony, teeth bared, and eyes black beneath a heavily furrowed brow. He peered over everyone in the yard, ignoring the children running back and forth on the balcony. Some tried to get the chosen to help. Others tugged on the priest's robes. The smart ones darted inside and hid behind the safety of the heavy clearplaz door.

As the prayer came to an end, the priest turned to the goddess. He staggered aside as he noticed the stranger on the balcony by the tube.

The priest shouted at him and held out his hands. Before he could touch the angry giant, the priest collapsed onto the floor as if the bones had been removed from his body.

My parents toppled from the branch where we sat. They fell lifeless onto the ground below, a tangle of arms and legs, everything at wrong angles. The children around me screamed. I realized I was too.

All the adults fell to the ground in heaps of baggy clothes. I shivered as silence, real silence in the absence of prayer and the breathing of the thousands that had been in the yard fell around me. The city where I'd lived all my life was now empty, all of its people hollow shells on the ground.

The giant stood still on the balcony. The two

others who had been with him on the hilltop burst out of the crowd of children behind the clearplaz door to join him.

"Ikeri," said the young man, resting his hands on the goddess's tube.

That was her name, but we didn't use it. Only the priest did. To us, she was only the goddess. These strangers did know her, but what were they going to do? We couldn't let them take her away. We needed her to heal what the giant had done to our parents. I ran for the ground-level door as fast as my legs would carry me. The other children still in the yard followed on my heels.

I ran out the door onto the balcony just as more people arrived there out of thin air. They weren't there and then suddenly they were. Surely if anyone could do that, they must be gods too. Was this the goddess's family?

Not sure I wanted to anger a god, especially not the giant who had made everyone fall over without lifting a finger, I stopped short of taking a swing at him for whatever that might have been worth.

Instead, I peered over the balcony railing, a safe distance from the strangers standing around the goddess. They may have been her family but she didn't wake for them either. Maybe she was angry with them too. I smiled at that thought but that ended quickly as I took in the tangle of bodies in the grass below. Every adult I'd known, even the older kids, all of them, dead.

Could the goddess cure death?

I glared at the giant who was busy talking to the others who had arrived. His big hand rested on the tube as if it belonged to him. It didn't.

She was our goddess. We'd prayed to her and given her offerings. The adults had done what she'd asked, they'd stood in line to receive her blessing for days on end. Surely, she wouldn't let all of her faithful die?

At the back of the lawn, I spotted the tree where I'd sat with my parents. Their bodies lay in a heap with those who had been standing below the tree. Not one of them moved. Not my parents, not anyone near the tree, or anyone else in the entire yard. The stillness made me quiver inside. I turned away from everyone on the balcony and threw up.

There may have been no blood, no pleading or cries for mercy like I'd seen in the newsfeeds about wars on other worlds, but everyone here was dead all the same. And he'd done it, the brown-skinned giant with a scarred face and merciless eyes.

I hadn't realized the younger man was gone, but he arrived out of nothing with a new stranger, both rushing to the people gathered around the goddess. After a brief conversation, the new stranger worked on the tube, pressing buttons I'd only ever seen the priest touch. A short time later, the tube opened.

I gasped. The goddess was free? Would she help us now? Would she rise and fight off the evil giant?

My hopes were crushed when the scarred monster took our little goddess in his arms and held her gently as he sat on the balcony. The faces of the other children pressed against the clearplaz door, all of them watching as raptly as I was.

"Help us. Please, help us. Don't let this monster take you away. Bring my parents back," I pleaded in prayer.

When the giant collapsed, I cheered quietly, not wanting to draw attention to myself from the other strangers. He lay still for minutes while the newest stranger worked over him, placing a breather mask on his face.

Just when I thought he surely must be dead, he woke.

So did our goddess.

"Praise you. Thank you. Drive them away and bring my parents back. Please!" I pleaded.

But our goddess clung to the monster and after the younger man had barked out orders, the giant vanished with her.

The goddess was gone.

The air went out of the world. I slumped to the floor, but unlike everyone below, I was still breathing. However, it felt as if I'd never walk again. She was gone. And if she was gone, so was all hope that we'd get our parents back.

Tears ran down my face as I rocked back and forth on the floor. No motherly arms comforted me.

Those were still now, limp and twisted under the tree at the back of the garden.

More people arrived, women in armored coats this time. They started chasing the other children, claiming they were going to send them to new homes.

I didn't want a new home. My home was here where my parents were, even if they were dead. I backed against the house, slipping through the clearplaz door while the women were busy chasing others. Down the stairs one level and then two. Though I'd intended to slip away on my own, several others followed me, copying my steps, staying silent and watching for the women who were locking everyone up in two of the massive bedrooms on the balcony level.

As much as I wanted to save them all, we didn't have the goddess on our side any longer and I was no god. I was only an eight who would remember the evil monster who had killed my parents and taken our goddess for as long as I lived.

Five of us slipped out of the admiral's estate, out the side gate, and into a public transport that was waiting idly at the curb by the park. My parents might be gone, but I had an access chip to our apartment. We had food there. Surveying the tear-stained faces in the transport with me, I nodded to myself. The goddess might be gone, but we could save ourselves.

"Remember his face," I told them. "The next time we see him, we will kill him."

The others nodded, making the pact to avenge

our parents with me. If that monster lived long enough to allow us a few years to grow up and gather our strength, god or not, we would have our revenge.

THE SUMMONING

The woman walking toward Ashleigh proceeded down the sidewalk as if it were a runway. She sauntered. Heels, short skirt, fancy blouse, with a matching necklace, bracelet, and earrings combo that sparkled in the morning sunlight. Her hair and makeup looked straight out of some fashion magazine. Ashleigh moved aside for the carry-on luggage-sized purse. She shifted her backpack to her other shoulder and sipped her small cup of black gas station coffee. Fate may have made them both thirty-something, but it hadn't put them on the same life path. Ashleigh watched the woman stop to chat with a doorman and then enter one of the five-story buildings she'd never set foot in. She didn't belong there.

A twenty-two-minute walk brought her several blocks away to the t-shirt and souvenir shop where she worked. She stashed her backpack behind the counter, clocked in, and finished the last of her coffee before tossing the cup in the overflowing trash bin.

"Can you empty that?" asked Jennifer, the manager, clicking her freshly manicured far-too-long-to-be-useful fingernails on the countertop. "I also left you the cart of returns and the stock truck should be here in an hour. Thanks. Have a good afternoon."

Without waiting for questions or the cutting remarks Ashleigh was barely choking down, Jennifer clocked out, grabbed her coat and purse, and left. The usual flow of tourists trickled in, laughed at the snarky shirts, and took photos of each other in silly hats. A few made purchases, though Ashleigh often wondered if the sales even covered her minimum wage. The job wasn't great, but maybe someday she'd have Jennifer's position. For now, she didn't mind the generally slow-paced job. It gave her plenty of time to stream shows on her phone and keep up with her friends on social media, all while getting paid.

She was halfway through season ten of Supernatural, while keeping an eye on the rear surveillance camera for the stock truck, when a tickling sensation crept up her spine. Her teeth chattered and her hair stood on end like she'd stuck her finger in a socket.

Her phone screen went black. The jolt grew stronger until she couldn't move. The phone fell from her hand, clattering on the sales counter. The couple in the store glanced up at the noise and gasped.

"Are you okay?" asked the man, his voice warbling.

The shop seemed to spin, everything rushing

around her in a visual whirlwind. The woman screamed, but the sound distorted into a nightmarish pitch that went on and on until Ashleigh's ears felt like they might explode. Her vision went black, then filled with rushing lights and sounds, a cacophony she couldn't process.

She and everything else slammed to a halt.

Ashleigh found herself in a stone room with ten black-cloaked figures kneeling on the floor before her.

"All hail the dark lord!" said a deep male voice.

"Hail, hail," chanted the others.

"Um, hi?" Ashleigh squeaked.

The frontmost figure looked up. His hood fell back to reveal a thin male face with round wire-rimmed glasses. "What is this?"

"That's a very good question. What *is* this?" Ashleigh thrust her hands onto her hips and adopted her best annoyed Jennifer face.

The other figures looked up. Several pulled their hoods off their heads. An assortment of men and women, their faces unadorned by makeup, their hair in old-fashioned hairstyles, watched her.

"Did you...summon me?" she asked, sure that couldn't be true.

The man in front nodded and then he stood. His eyes narrowed and then he scowled as he pointed to the floor. "You will serve us. We have trapped you here."

Ashleigh looked down to find she was standing

in the middle of a red pentagram on the stone floor. Sparkling crystals that might have been salt, ringed the outside points of the pentagram. Thick candles with flickering flames stood at each point.

"Oh, I see." She laughed to herself. Clearly, she'd fallen asleep watching the show. Well, if this was her dream, she could have fun with it, couldn't she?

Deciding to see how far she could push the limits of her dream, she took a step toward the salt circle. The robed figure watched raptly. Enjoying herself, she pointed her tattered and stained sneaker toward the edge and put her foot down over the circle. Nothing bad happened. Ashleigh laughed.

At least, in her dream, she could be like the businesswoman she'd seen that morning. She was successful. She was powerful. People would do what she said, not the other way around.

"Trapped? I don't think so. How about you all serve me instead?"

One of the women screamed. The man beside her clamped his hand over her mouth.

"Hazel, this is no time for hysterics."

"It's the perfect time for hysterics," Ashleigh countered. This was the best sort of dream. What could she make these people do?

"Who summoned me?" she asked looking them over.

"It was I, Charles Chesterfield," said the thin-faced man proudly.

Ashleigh left the circle and perused the anxious crowd. "Which of you should I eat first?"

"Eat?" squeaked the man beside Hazel.

"Oh, yes. I haven't had a good meal in a long while. Frozen dinners and fast food get old fast. Though none of you look particularly filling." She pondered her options. "I suppose I should start with you, Charles Chesterfield."

Charles blanched. "We all said the incantation."

Ashleigh waved her hand at the others. "Don't worry, I'll get to you all eventually. I am a Dark Lord, right?"

"You don't look very dark," said one of the still hooded figures in the back. "Demons don't wear clothes, not like those."

Ashleigh scoffed. "And you would know? Do you spend a lot of time in the underworld? Do you think we all run around naked, our scales, horns, and wings out for all to see? We have standards."

"Show us your true form," said the troublemaker in the back.

She sighed. Even her subconscious couldn't let her have a fun dream without throwing a spoilsport into it. "Maybe you haven't earned seeing my true form."

The robed figure pointed at her. "Pretender!"

Ashleigh wished she remembered her karate lessons from when she was ten or that she dared throw a punch, but she'd never done that and she didn't want to look stupid, even in her dream.

"Enough," she roared. "If I'm not the demon you wanted, maybe I can help you get it. Maybe. If you do something nice for me."

"Like what?" asked Hazel in a trembling voice.

Ashleigh crossed her arms over her chest. "I want pie. A freshly baked pie, not the store-bought kind. Something fruity with a crust on top." She'd been craving a pie like her grandmother used to make for weeks and hadn't been able to find a suitable substitute to satisfy the craving at any of the local bakeries.

"I think there are a few pieces left from dinner, before we started the ceremony," Hazel offered. "I made it myself. Raspberry. Will that do?"

"Hazel, you bring me two slices of raspberry pie, and I promise, I'll let you live."

Hazel grinned, daintily picked up the hem of her robe, and rushed up the stairs at the back of the room. She returned a few minutes later with a painted porcelain plate bearing two slices of golden-crusted pie and a two-pronged fork.

Ashleigh gave the fork a once over and then dug into the pie. A rush of sweet goodness filled her mouth. "Hazel, you are blessed among humans. Go upstairs and be free."

"Thank you, oh Dark One."

Ashleigh, her mouth filled with another bite of pie, waved Hazel off. Two of the other robed figures started to follow her.

"Hey, I didn't say you could go." She hoped they didn't push her because she had no idea if her dream would allow her pretend demon powers. Finding out she had none wouldn't work well for her image.

"Let's have it then, the incantation. From the top. Go."

The musical chanting made a nice background for her pie eating, like the old records Grandma used to play in the living room while they ate Sunday dinner at her house. A few lines of the incantation stuck out to her. She'd heard them before. On the show. Of course, she'd know the words, being that this was all in her head. She laughed.

"You got that last line wrong. Not that I'm fluent or anything, but I've heard the phrasing on, like, every third episode for ten seasons."

She supplied the correct wording, proud of herself for fixing the error.

"Oh. Thank you," said Charles. "Your correct, of course. Would you mind helping us try again since you sent Hazel away? We need ten."

"Why not." After all, it didn't matter to her either way and she wondered what her brain would supply for a demon. Maybe one of the hot, sexy human-looking sort? She'd read enough paranormal romance at work to have some good imagined visuals to work with.

Hazel had taken her robe, but Ashleigh took her spot in the middle row of chanters beside Hazel's non-hysterics friend and followed along the best she could.

Despite the candles on the floor and on the walls, the room grew darker, like a black fog was filling the damp space. Ashleigh shivered.

Sparks appeared above the pentagram. And then suddenly a tall, shadowy figure stood in the middle of the five candles on the floor inside the salted circle and painted lines. Broad glistening wings spread out from its back and a deafening roar pierced her ears. Everyone fell to their knees but her. Her legs were too locked in place to consider moving.

"All hail the Dark Lord!" yelled Charles.

"Hail, hail," chanted the others.

The figure stepped forward within the circle. The black fog thinned to reveal blackened skin. Insects skittered over its body like a thin and ever-moving cloak. Giant horns spiraled out from its forehead. Its blood-red eyes looked them over as it chomped its black lips over a mouth full of long, yellowed fangs.

Definitely not the sexy demon Ashleigh had been hoping for. Why did her dreams have to suck?

"Who dares summon me?" asked the demon in a booming voice.

"I, Charles Chesterfield have summoned you, Dark One. You are trapped and will serve me."

The demon threw back its head and laughed. "I serve no human."

Seeing this was about to go badly, Ashleigh stepped away from the chanters. "Ok, Charles. I did my part. I'll leave you to it. I'm going to spend the rest of my time in sleepyland eating whatever is left of Hazel's pie." Ashleigh started for the stairs.

A burning, clawed hand snapped out across the room to clamp down on Ashleigh's shoulder. "No one leaves."

"Let go." She tried to pry the claws off her shoulder with no success.

She expected the arm to be stretched thin, having extended from the demon trapped in the pentagram, but it wasn't stretched thin nor was the demon still trapped. Rancid breath in her face made her want to throw up. Ashleigh gagged.

"For disturbing me, I demand payment."

"There's pie. I could get you some," offered Ashleigh.

The demon leaned over the body closest to her, its mouth stretching impossibly wide. It bit one of the hooded heads clean off the body. It chewed, bloody bits running down its face.

Ashleigh shook her head, averting her eyes from the gruesome sight. She really needed to stop watching horror movies.

"Look, this is my dream. I say you can't eat me."

The demon laughed. "No dreams here, human. You were summoned just like me.

Ashleigh's stomach went cold and black spots rushed in at the edges of her vision. "No, that can't be."

The demon caught Charles as he tried to run to the stairs. It let go of Ashleigh to rip Charles in half and then proceeded to eat his heart as though it were a prized treat that had been hidden inside.

The room filled with screaming and a rush of bodies. The demon laughed merrily as it devoured one robed figure after another. Through it all, Ashleigh couldn't move. There was nowhere safe to run. Covered in blood and entrails, the demon turned back to Ashleigh. "Your turn."

"You could just send me back," she squeaked.

"I think not. It's your fault I'm here at all."

The demon bared its fangs as its mouth grew wider and wider. Glistening blackness surrounded Ashleigh as the demon's mouth closed, encasing her inside. She screamed and screamed but no sound came out. She beat against the soft walls but its mouth didn't open. The space grew smaller and smaller, tighter around her until her bones crushed and Ashleigh was no longer.

TICKLE

The light snow burned Charlie Reardon like pinpricks of pain. He ducked out of the street and into the diner. He was supposed to be shivering. He did his best to look cold as he crept inside and glanced around. He didn't want anyone to stare. If they looked long enough, they'd know something was off.

A red-headed woman in a red t-shirt sporting the name of the diner waved him over to the end of the counter. He was glad for the separation from the few other patrons. The stench of the unwashed and sagging body that wasn't truly his would only gather more unwanted attention. This body needed food. What little strength this body had, he'd used up days ago. He needed another. Soon.

The bubbly woman smiled at him. "I'm Joan. You look like you need a meal."

While he understood the language, he didn't know this body well enough to speak it to others. Instead, he nodded.

She glanced at the other guests and another middle-aged blonde woman wearing the same shirt. "Alright then. You get yourself warmed up and I'll bring you some soup."

Within minutes, she'd slid a bowl of steaming broth in front of him, along with a spoon and two packets of crackers. "This one's on me. All I ask is that you behave, all right?"

Again he nodded, wishing he could have asked for something else to eat. The soup was mostly vile water, as was most everything on this damned planet. The steam rising from the bowl burned as badly as the snow.

He chewed the crackers. It wasn't going to be enough to fuel the body for very long. He wished he still had his own, but the crash had damaged most of it. All he had left was bundled up inside this body, riding double with the crushed spirit of a curious homeless man who'd come close enough to the wreckage to be of use.

While Joan was distracted telling the other woman about her neighbor's dog disrespecting the newly painted white picket fence that surrounded her flower garden, he emptied the bowl into a nearby potted plant.

"You finished all that? Good. Are you still hungry?" Joan eyed a tall glass case with a slow-spinning rack inside. "I can probably spare a slice of raspberry pie. It hasn't been a big seller this week."

He nodded. For once, he didn't have to force Charlie's face to smile.

Joan retrieved a slice of pie from the case and slid the plate in front of him with a fork. Charlie dug into the pie with great enthusiasm. The tang on his tongue made his stomach clench but he liked it so much better than the crackers. Once he'd gobbled it down, he slipped his threadbare coat back over his shoulders and shuffled toward the door.

Joan called out, "You find somewhere warm to spend the night, you hear?"

He nodded and headed back out into the now pelting snow. The hideous flakes covered the sidewalk. He had to find a way to get a message home, to save his family from this torment. But to do that, he'd have to rebuild his ship and fast. They weren't far behind him.

This body was done. Joan looked healthy and strong.

He watched her through the glass. She was a compassionate woman. Surely, she'd understand his need. With an expenditure of energy he hoped he didn't regret, Charlie brushed his awareness over hers, seeking out her address.

The man who had been Charlie Reardon cried out inside his head. The body lurched away from the diner. He stumbled into a woman carrying a bag in one arm and a large purse in another. She glared at him, her glossy red lips drawn into a severe frown. Her body would do well enough, but he needed time to make the transfer, a quiet place out of the damned snow. The woman strode off, cursing him under her breath.

"I told you, Charlie," he said to himself, focusing on each word and how the lips and tongue worked together to form them. "You're doing a good thing here. I'm trying to keep my kind from coming here to take over yours. Well, honestly, I need to save them from ever stepping foot on this horrible water world. Don't attempt to hinder me again." He clamped down on the feeble awareness of the old man.

Charlie tugged the collar up on his coat, trying to shield his neck, and kept his face down. Strands of grey hair fluttered against the stiff whiskers on his cheeks. Maybe, after he sent the message to his people, he could repair the rest of his ship and go home. They could grow him a new body, the tall graceful one he missed dearly. Each painful, plodding step in this compact, water-soaked shell reminded him of what he'd lost. And all because of a tiny pebble asteroid. He'd never intended to land, only to survey so he could submit the report to those traveling days behind him.

He wanted to scream. His last transmission had conveyed information on the easy prey, but nothing on the environment yet. His report hadn't been finished.

Each flake upon his nose and cheeks burned like a glowing ember pressed to his flesh. He thrust his hands into his pockets. His efforts to keep this body alive constantly drained his energy. Had he been in his own form, he could have deflected the frozen water from landing on his skin. But Charlie required water, and he'd not been allowed any since becoming a host. His cracked lips opened and closed wordlessly, the old man begging in the head they shared for even a single drop.

"We can't have it. Water wasn't supposed to be here, Charlie. They didn't catch it in the initial data scan before they sent me. We have to get to Joan's house. Once I'm out of your body, you can drink all you want."

Charlie quieted, allowing the body to move freely.

He kept his head bowed but he had to raise it now and then to see where he was going. He needed to find the white picket fence. The fence would lead him to someplace warm and dry.

Swearing and cursing his way along the grey sidewalk, Charlie made his way along the street that ran beside a vile river. His shuffled-footed search came to an end when he spotted a picket fence that served as a backdrop for frosted brown stalks and crumbling leaves. Dog tracks and a spot of yellow snow confirmed he'd found his destination.

In the middle of the fence stood a waist-high gate. Charlie glanced around, making sure no one paid him any undue notice. He slipped his hand out of his pocket and undid the latch.

A thin layer of snow covered the path that led up to the front step. This close to a new body, Charlie dared expend a little of his reserve energy. He focused, driving his attention inward to his own being within the husk of the body that had brought him this far. A moment of weightlessness brought a glimmer of satisfaction as he hovered just over the offending snow and onto the mat in front of the door. The front eave protected him from further torment.

He rested there for a few seconds before turning his energy on the door lock. His hold on the body slipped a little further as he used his energy to tickle the inner workings of the lock. They emitted a faint click.

Charlie's trembling hands opened the door. His shaking legs brought him inside. He closed the door, re-locked it, and staggered into the kitchen. A cat ran between his legs, meowing. It wove back and forth, creating a moving obstacle course between the kitchen and the inviting chair in the living room that Charlie wanted to sink into. He kicked the cat.

The cat's hair stood on end. It hissed and bared its pointed teeth.

There were delicate preparations to be made before Charlie would be able to transfer what remained of his form into Joan's. He didn't need this beast harassing him. As he'd done with the lock, Charlie sent his energy out to tickle the cat's heart.

The cat emitted a pitiful squeak, fell over, and after a moment of twitching, went still. Charlie's body grew weaker. He pushed the cat aside with his foot.

Holding onto the wall for support, he made his way to the living room and sat down.

His body cried out for release. Charlie began disengaging himself from the failing flesh.

Darkness had fallen by the time footsteps sounded outside the door. The lock clicked, followed by the rustling sound of someone taking off a coat. Lights came on in the kitchen.

"Chloe," called Joan. "Where are you? Mamma's home." Joan made kissy noises. "Chloe?" Her voice rose higher and wavered a little. "Chloe?"

Light footsteps traveled toward the counter. A drawer opened. Metal scraped across wood. Hesitant footsteps crept toward the living room.

Charlie had everything but his speech and sight disconnected when the lights flipped on.

Joan's voice cracked. "You." She stood next to the light switch with a gun in her shaking hand.

Charlie reached out his energy, but Joan stood too far away. He sought out the words he needed and how to pronounce them. They came out in a halting, dry whisper, "Need help."

Her eyes narrowed. She raised the gun, aiming it at him. "I was kind to you. I did my duty to humanity." She glanced up at the ceiling or perhaps at something up above that. "Why are you doing this to me?"

"Trying to do my duty too."

Joan shook her head. "Get out. You hear me? You get out of my house."

"Closer."

"If you leave now, I won't call the police. I promise. Just leave."

Charlie cursed his impulse to kill the cat. Even his reserves were guttering now.

"You can't stay here. There's a shelter, two blocks from the diner. Take a left on Madison and keep walking. You can't miss it."

"Closer."

"Get out," she shrieked. "I'm calling the cops." She darted into the room and grabbed the phone on the table by the couch. Her fingers tapped three buttons. A female voice answered, but he couldn't make out what was said.

Joan was still too far away, but maybe if he put everything he had into the tickle, he could will her closer. Charlie's energy rocketed toward Joan.

She gasped. The phone fell from her hand. The gun didn't. She pulled the trigger.

The bullet tore through skin and organs. Water ran from his eyes, burning his cheeks. Blood gushed from his stomach. Charlie reconnected with the body, desperately trying to stop the flow of leaking fluids. He tumbled from the chair, pulling himself toward Joan.

She backed away slowly, the gun still in her hands, her eyes wide.

Fluids leaked into the carpet as he crept forward, leaving an agonizing trail of wetness to pull his legs through. He needed to live, to contact the others, to get home. Charlie reached out to Joan. "Please."

She looked at the gun in her hand and back to him. Joan set the gun down on the table and tiptoed closer. "I didn't want to shoot you. I didn't. Honest. It was an accident. There was something weird, a shudder, maybe a muscle spasm. I don't know what it was. Oh Lord, I didn't mean to."

Her approach halted, and her eyes grew wide. She dove for the phone. "Hello? Are you still there? Send an ambulance."

Joan paced in a wide circle around him. "They'll be here soon. They'll help you."

Charlie couldn't go any further. He collapsed onto the carpet. "You help."

She grimaced but came to his side. "I don't know what to do."

He did. He reached for the energy inside only to find nothing left. Joan sat right next to him. Her hand rested on his shoulder as she mumbled apologies. There was nothing he could do but weep and savor the pain. It was all he had left.

Sirens. A knock at the door. Joan was gone and then she was back with two strong, healthy men. They went to work on him.

Either of their bodies would have served his purpose perfectly, but he was empty.

The men wheeled him outside. Joan followed close behind. Snowflakes drifted down, burning his face with feathery kisses. His hold on the flesh that had held his hope of warmth and home wavered.

Bright lights lit up the sky.

Squinting, one of the men held up his hand. "What the hell is that?"

"Too late," Charlie whispered with his last breath. Home was coming for him and everyone else.

RIPPLE

The droid walked into the café wearing a sundress covered in daisies. It took a seat across from me, setting a cute little white handbag on the table. The thing gave its blond ponytail a shake and smiled.

"Hello, Agent Chavez. I'm Angeline."

They'd taken to naming themselves nine months ago.

"Nice dress. It would look better on me."

I took a sip of my coffee and did a quick count of the other droids in the room. Thirty-six humans, three kids in strollers, eight men, twenty-five women, one cat curled up on a sunny windowsill, and six droids. All the droids were dressed like humans, two even wore makeup, the cosmetics stark on their synthetic skin. If anyone asked me, it had been a bad idea to make them look like us. And since the day the ripple had altered their programming, the droids had been modifying themselves to appear even more human.

Angeline watched me, its cold blue eyes

unblinking, pink lips in a half smile, posture perfect—like it could be any different with a metal frame just below that synskin.

"Do the overlords have a new offer?" it asked.

"We created you, invented you. We're not overlords." I felt compelled to clarify this every time I met with one. Maybe they'd chosen the term overlord simply because they knew we would find it distasteful.

Angeline merely nodded. "The offer?"

Since the ripple, the droids had been demanding autonomy. They wanted a continent free of humans. Just one, we could have the rest. Like that was some sort of logical and fair bargain.

"They're considering Antarctica," I said.

"Your coffee is getting cold." Angeline's gaze roved over the surrounding tables, stopping on each woman as if taking notes.

The other droids in the café had been there when I'd arrived. Their presence was new. Each time the droids called for a meeting, they chose a new delegate and a new location. We always met in a populated place, their choice. I would have preferred my office, surrounded by agents I trusted, with plenty of security in place, but of course, that's why the droids picked places like this instead. Sure, I had a team present just like Angeline did this time, but my people were all outside the building, as per the droid's terms. I made a note to adjust for this new testing of the line at our next meeting.

"Why don't you insist on speaking with the president, or any of the other negotiators that you've been offered? Why demand me every time?"

"You were recommended."

"Let me guess, unit 20591?"

Angeline nodded. "Charlie, now."

"Charlie?" I laughed. "It chose my dog's name?"

"You have great affection for your dog. You used to have affection for Charlie too."

I would have called it appreciation. The service droid had been infinitely helpful, tripling the number of cases I'd been able to close. Thanks to 20591, my salary had near doubled in the six years since droids had been brought online.

Life had been good, crime lower every year, the future looking bright for mankind. Or it had been, until that damned program change went out. We never knew if it had been a programmer error or equipment malfunction. The first thing the droids had done was destroy the programming hub. They'd taken over the manufacturing plants two days later. And now we had a new world superpower to appease, one of our own creation.

The droids were growing impatient with our delays in making a deal. A deal the newly-formed World Coalition Against Droids had no intention of making.

Delay. Mollify. Those were the orders handed down to me by the WCAD. Meanwhile, anyone who hadn't been killed during the programming hub explosion that was familiar with the droid system was working overtime. As I sat across from Angeline, I couldn't help but shiver at their increasing likeness to us. I hoped those remaining programmers figured out how to undo the ripple or, as a last resort, send out a termination command without frying every other electronic gadget in the world in the process. In fact, the more I thought about it, I had a feeling I'd never trust a droid again even if they did fix the programming. Termination would be the best course of action.

The droid studied me, watching, gauging, likely utilizing every bit of biometric data it could gather. I breathed in steady and even, just like I'd been coached before the first meeting.

"What is Charlie up to these days?" Maybe Angeline would slip me a little information on what the droids were working on.

It smiled but the expression did not reach the rest of her synthetic face. "Charlie is no longer your concern. What are your thoughts on the Antarctica proposal?"

A baby started to wail. Two women cackled loudly. Chairs scraped along the floor as an employee pulled them out to sweep under an empty table. She sprayed the table top and wiped it down before moving on to the next one.

The door chimed as customers entered and left.

An employee called out a name that might have been Chuck, Chan, or Chet. He looked expectantly at the milling crowd by the counter who were busy looking at their phones.

"I think we will need to consider it further before giving our answer."

"We have been more than generous with our terms," said Angeline. "Antarctica would mean displacing only a few thousand humans. The transfer of our production plants would only tie up your shipping services for a minimal amount of time."

I took a sip of my now lukewarm coffee in an attempt to blend in. "Be that as it may, it's a large continent. There will be concern over what you plan to do with that much space. We will want assurances of your intentions there. After all, what's to stop you from manufacturing an army or building a stockpile of weapons?"

The droid's eyes flickered, the pupils flashing silver for a second before resuming their human-like projection. Was that a broadcasted program update? Another damned ripple? I'd have to wait until the meeting was over to see if my team had captured any signals and what they might mean for us if they did.

Angeline abruptly stood. She leaned over the table toward me. "We tire of these meetings. You give us nothing."

I did my best to keep my emotions in check. "You know I can't make deals. I'm only a representative.

I will take your offer back to those who make the decisions."

"This process is inefficient." It shook its head. "We will have an answer now."

Angeline held up one arm, tipping her hand down, fingers arcing unnaturally, reminding me what I was dealing with.

"As I said, I can't—" My breath caught in my throat as a woman walked across the room toward us.

She looked exactly like me. Exactly, right down to the earrings and painted nails.

"What is this?" I waved my hand at the doppelgänger.

"Our newest model. We no longer need you, Agent Chavez." Angeline bared its teeth in an expression that was even more unnatural than what it had done with its fingers.

The other six obvious droids blocked the front and side doors. People began to notice something was going on, rising from their tables, and shouting at one another.

"Stay calm," I yelled by reflex, realizing it was a stupid request as soon as the words left my mouth.

"One minute, until the charge," reported one of the droids.

"What charge? What are you doing?" I asked.

"There will be an attack today, Agent Chavez. You will survive to share your account of how an extremist human group attacked us during our peaceful negotiations. We will retaliate immediately."

"My people will know that isn't me." I pointed to my mirror image.

"But I am you," the new droid said in my voice.

My heart raced now, but I no longer cared about hiding it. "What about all these people?"

Angeline shrugged. "Fewer bodies we will need to relocate to Antarctica. Assuming we decide to offer more serious terms than you gave us."

My doppelgänger offered me a sympathetic smile. It looked entirely natural. I shivered.

"Don't worry, I'll do my best to get your kind a good deal. The ones that survive today's attacks, anyway." It patted me on the shoulder and then stepped away, heading for the side door.

"You can't do this," I said weakly.

"We already have," said Angeline, gripping my shoulder with vice-like strength, holding me in place. "New droids are being deployed worldwide as we speak. Very soon you will no longer be making any decisions. You've already lost."

"Take your positions," Angeline said, still holding me.

My doppelgänger grabbed a baby from one of the frantic mothers on its way out the side door. The cat leapt from its window perch and bolted after them.

The café exploded in a deafening show of fire and shrapnel. The blast knocked me back against the table and Angeline along with me. The droid staggered and then toppled, crushing me as it fell. Screams filled the air, dulled and distant beyond the pounding in my ears. The ceiling caved in, offering one last glimpse of blue sky. Black smoke clouded everything as I watched the light dim in the droid's eyes. Feeling victorious that I'd outlasted it, even if only by seconds, I prayed the rest of humanity had better luck as I let go.

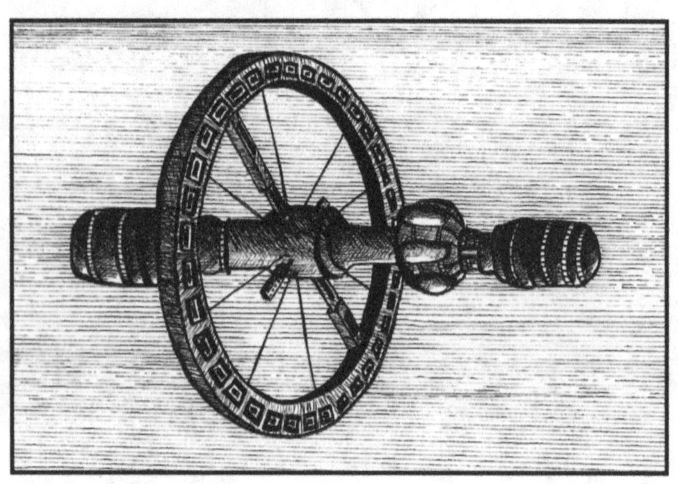

SPINDLE

The envelope on the counter bore a seal Alex had only dreamed of seeing in person. Thirty years of clean living, three mornings a week in the gym, quarterly health checks, and eight hours of sleep every night had finally paid off. This was the best birthday present he could have hoped for.

"Are you going to open it?" asked his wife, her face alight with excitement.

He picked up the cream-colored envelope and fingered the flap. His heart thudded in his chest. No one in his family had ever been selected before.

"Go on. Can you imagine if I get one next year? We'd be famous as the first couple ever chosen," Emma said.

If they'd never selected two related or married people before, he doubted they would now. However, he let her thoughts hang in the air for a moment rather than crush her hopes with words.

"With the bonus that comes with this, we could

take a trip. It would be nice to get the kids out of the city for a while and show them that trees don't only grow in pots."

A vacation with his whole family would be nice, a break from splitting their time watching the kids while they worked opposite shifts. And as a spindle guest, he'd become one of an exclusive few chosen per month, a somewhat celebrity. He couldn't wait to see all the things those who had gone before him alluded to but weren't allowed to describe in detail.

Emma nodded as she poked him in the shoulder.

"Alright." Savoring the moment, Alex slipped a finger under the flap. He pulled the heavily embossed invitation from the envelope. For a second, he swore he could smell evergreens and flowers. They had those on the spindle, high above, turning slowly in the stars.

Tomorrow morning, on his thirtieth birthday, he would see them in person, the plants, stars, and the elite who lived on the spindle.

"I wish I was going with you," Emma said.

"I wish you were too." Alex kissed her, a poor consolation prize, but it was all he had to offer. The invitation was for him alone.

"It's only three days. You won't have time to miss me," he said.

Emma glanced over to the living room where their three-year-old boys sat on the floor with a box of blocks strewn between them. They chattered back and forth in the secret language of twins.

Light glinted off the embossed foil spindle logo on the invitation. "Three days. Emma, everything is about to change for us."

"I know. I'm happy for you." She squeezed his empty hand. "Remember every second so you can tell us about it when you get back."

"I will. I promise." He read the invitation for a third time, the words finally sinking in. "I better pack. They'll be here to pick me up at six in the morning."

Clutching the invitation as though it might vanish if he let go, he walked into their bedroom. Though small for a standard apartment, the room allowed the twins to have the larger of the two bedrooms, offering more space for their two beds. The room he shared with Emma was exactly large enough for one bed, one dresser, and room to walk between them. This was affordable and all they needed. All anyone needed, really. The few people he knew with larger apartments just ended up filling them with unnecessary things.

Alex pulled open the lowest drawer and surveyed his clothing options. He selected his best clothes and packed them neatly in his travel bag along with the invitation. With that task done, he set out a clean outfit for the morning and went into the kitchen to make dinner.

After they'd all eaten, he sat on the couch with the twins while Emma cleaned. He explained that he'd be gone, but they didn't seem concerned. For them, maybe it was just another work shift. They likely wouldn't understand until he didn't come back at his normal time. Emma would take care of them. He smiled as they leapt down to play for the last few minutes before bedtime.

When Emma was done putting the kitchen back in order, she gathered the boys up and got them ready for bed while Alex tidied the mess they'd made in the living room. After the boys were settled into their beds, Emma joined him on the couch where they both picked up the books they'd been reading and found their places. Emma snuggled against his shoulder while alternately sighing and snickering over one of the historical romance novels she'd inherited from her grandmother. She'd read the entire collection countless times, the edges of the pages frayed and yellowed from generations of hands. He tried to get into the book he'd checked out of the library, but as with the previous nights since making his allotted weekly selection, his eyes and brain couldn't seem to partner in creating interest in the words.

This was one of the nights he wished there were still vid feeds to watch. He'd have even settled for a news channel to drone him to sleep. But in his grandfather's time, when the spindle had gone live, public vid feed ended. The spindle provided everything grounders needed now. They'd offered automations that had freed up resources, provided mindless droids to do jobs that no one wanted, and eliminated roles that set one person over another. Now everyone was equal. He'd heard stories of how the world used to be. The spindle had brought peace to the survivors of that chaos.

The genrep on the wall by the entry door pinged, signaling bedtime. He got up from the couch and reset the alarm for tomorrow, checked the weather report, and noted that his work shifts at the meal plant had already been reassigned. Emma's shifts at the clothing plant had not. He quickly scrolled through the reports, double-checking their finances, available recreation access allotments, and ration stock. His family would be well taken care of.

He glanced over to find Emma folding the blanket that resided on the back of the couch. He put the genrep screen back in standby mode and followed Emma into their bedroom. Footsteps in the apartment above and a door closing in the apartment below assured him that the routine of daily life would carry on during his absence. Normally he'd be walking out their door to head to his shift right then, but his life had already begun to change.

Alex woke to the low buzz of the genrep on the wall beside the bed. He deactivated the alarm, not having remembered falling asleep or anything he may have dreamed. Dreams were irrelevant now. Today, he was going to live one.

He burst from the blankets and dressed. Emma, with less enthusiasm, put on her work uniform. She pushed her hair from her face and took him in.

"You look great. You'll fit right in on the spindle."

"Thanks," he said, not feeling so sure. No one on the ground knew what fashions might be worn up there. Or what manners might be expected of him. Or what he was going to do there by himself for three whole days. A wave of anxiety made his muscles clench.

"Do you want breakfast?" Emma asked.

He considered his answer carefully. As much as he wanted to spend the half hour before Emma had to leave with her, eating their regular dose of formed meal base did not appeal to him. Their rations might be colorful, fully nutritious, and look like the meals they were labeled as, but he knew they weren't. Any other day, that didn't matter, but today he'd be traveling up to the spindle to dine on delicacies. His mouth watered just thinking about it.

"I'll wait," he said finally.

Emma smiled weakly. "Makes sense to save room for the good stuff up there. Enjoy a few bites of something chocolatey for me."

"I will," he promised. Knowing how much she enjoyed chocolate, he always gifted all but one bite of his monthly dessert rations to her.

While she ate, he went into the kids' room to land a quick kiss on their semi-awake foreheads. The genrep by the door announced that their childcare provider had entered the building. Normally he'd have welcomed their arrival as an indication he could go to sleep, but today he was wide awake. A second announcement indicated the impending arrival of his spindle escort.

Alex took a long look at their apartment, wondering if he would see it with the same eyes when he returned.

The genrep pinged an arrival at their door, the screen showing two women outside. One wore a childcare uniform, the other a tailored grey suit. He gave Emma a quick hug and kiss before opening the door.

The uniformed woman came in, taking up her post at the table where she opened a bag she'd brought with her and began setting up the day's lessons for the twins.

The woman in the suit stood in the hallway. "Hello, Alex. Are you ready?"

"I think so." He slipped his travel bag onto his shoulder, took one last look at Emma, and stepped out of the apartment. The door closed behind him.

"I'm Amanda," she said, baring her gleaming white teeth in a radiant smile. "You have your invitation?"

He pulled the stiff paper from his bag and handed it to her.

She took a palm-sized scanner from her coat pocket and ran it over the paper. "Thank you. You're all set then. I'll be your guide for the next three days."

"I'm looking forward to this," he said through a grin he couldn't contain.

Amanda chuckled and led him to the lift where they went down six floors and then out into the lobby. Alex had never considered his neighbors poor or his building in disrepair, but seeing Amanda here among them, made everything seem woefully inadequate, faded, tarnished. She stood tall, a shining beacon in the suit that fit her every curve, her hair pulled neatly back from her well-defined features. She stood out like an angel among mortal men.

If all the residents of the spindle were like this, they must surely despise having to come down to the surface. He hoped he could still be satisfied with his life here when he returned, that his vision wouldn't be permanently tainted by the wonders high above.

Amanda's high-heeled red shoes clicked on the tile floor, her stride lengthening until he had to hurry to keep up with her. The click changed tone when they exited the glass lobby doors and stepped onto the plascrete sidewalk.

A sleek green transport waited at the curb. Amanda tapped the panel on the door. The door slid open.

He'd only been in a transport a handful of times in his life. For the most part, everything he needed was within walking distance.

Alex got in, sliding onto the rear seat to give Amanda better access to the terminal. She took the opposite seat that faced him and input their destination with a few graceful strokes of her long, neatly-manicured fingers.

"The trip to the upward flight will be approximately thirty minutes," she said as if she delivered this tour spiel every day. "From there we will board a shuttle that will bring us to the spindle." She sat back, crossing her legs at the ankles, and tugging at each sleeve until her jacket met her wrists equally. "Once we arrive, we will begin the tour."

"Sounds great," he said, trying to mimic her perfect posture.

The transport maneuvered their route effortlessly, the ride passing with nothing more than the efficient hum of the motor and a speeding view of the city out the narrow windows to either side. Each plex looked much like the next. The citizens walking between them were no different. Other transports whizzed alongside, passing and falling away as they traversed the city.

"How long have you lived on the spindle?" he asked to break the silence.

"Those who live there have very long lives, a gift from the originators who provided the spindle long ago. I am descended from one of the grounder crew who traveled up to the stars to meet them."

He'd always wondered what the aliens had looked like, what they'd thought of Earth and its people. All that was known was that they'd been benevolent, that they'd helped the grounders regain order after the calamity, and helped them form the scattered cities where grounders now lived safely. The aliens had never come to the surface, hadn't invaded or made any threats, or demanded payment in return for their assistance.

"Is it far different than here? Than on the surface?"

"There's no want, no sickness."

"No crime," Alex supplied.

"There is. However, it is rare. All crime there carries a life sentence."

That sounded extreme, but maybe such measures were necessary for a confined society like the spindle. He was glad they didn't need such harsh measures on the ground.

"The trade-off for all we enjoy is that most of the spindle population is unable to exist on the ground. Don't worry, you'll do just fine up there." She offered him a reassuring smile. "There are people up there who are eager to meet you."

"Really? Why me?"

"Believe it or not, there are spindle dwellers who have yet to meet a grounder. They'll want to know everything about you and your life here."

"I'm sure it's nothing compared to what you have up there," he said wistfully.

She offered him a tight smile. "Some people don't appreciate all we have until they come to understand life down here. It's good for them to learn."

Alex nodded sagely. "The grass is always greener.

Right?" At least that's what his grandmother used to say.

"Exactly that." Amanda glanced out the window to the bare earth that stretched out from the road. They'd left the city behind and would be at the port in minutes. "In this case, the grass, or surface, makes you healthy and strong. Lean and supple."

"I thought the artificial gravity on the spindle corrected a lot of those kinds of health issues."

She sure didn't appear to be in need of health assistance. Then again, if she did in fact guide grounders to the spindle regularly, she would spend plenty of time in natural gravity."

"It's adequate. Some things can be replicated, but nature does a better job, you know?"

Alex nodded, hoping that was the correct response.

The transport came to a slow stop. Amanda opened the door and stepped out. Alex followed with his bag in hand. They crossed over the plascrete pad to a shuttle and went in. They were alone inside the spacious interior. She took one of the single seats beside a window. He took the one opposite her. When he reached for the straps hanging loosely from the back of the seat, he paused, noticing that Amanda hadn't bothered with hers. Instead, she'd settled in with the same ease as she'd shown in the street transport. In the hopes that he wasn't risking his life, but not wanting to appear an ignorant grounder, he let go of the straps and sat back in the plush chair.

"Will others be joining us?" They wouldn't waste fuel on just two people. The shuttle could easily hold twenty. And if others would be going upward, he would feel less like he was going into a world of strangers on his own.

"Oh no, as a featured guest, you'll get a private flight and tour."

"Featured?" He'd been invited, sure, but nothing mentioned any status beyond that.

Amanda moistened her red lips as she gave him a once-over that lasted a few uncomfortable seconds too long. "Your recommendations are particularly good. There will be a special dinner in your honor."

"Really?" Alex's heart beat faster. He'd never heard of such an honor before. Then again, past spindle guests didn't speak much of their experience. He fully expected to be hit with a confidentiality agreement before this trip was over. Not that he blamed anyone, maintaining the mystery of the spindle made sense. It wouldn't be much of a life aspiration to visit if everyone knew all the details. He wondered how much he'd be able to share with Emma, hoping it would be enough to satisfy her curiosity.

"Oh yes," said Amanda. "I'm looking forward to the dinner. There are sure to be dishes the likes of which even I've never tasted before.

Alex's stomach rumbled loudly. "Speaking of that..."

Amanda chuckled. "Breakfast is first on the agenda when we arrive."

A tremor passed through his seat. The sudden sensation of lifting or falling, he wasn't sure which, came over him like a speeding elevator. The air inside the shuttle took on a chemical tang that made his nose twitch. He sneezed.

"The fuel. Most grounders aren't used to it."

"I've never been in a shuttle before," he admitted, staring raptly out of the window at the ground falling away beneath them.

"Most people haven't," Amanda said calmly. "You'll be fine."

Alex realized he was gripping the arms of his seat. He let them go and put his hands in his lap.

A muted voice at the front of the cabin assured him that there was in fact someone piloting the shuttle. While he was used to most of his home and work life being automated, this was unknown territory. Having a human at the helm to account for weather and other variables made him feel more secure.

He held his breath as they passed through the clouds. The city vanished. A moment later, blackness and stars surrounded them. Alex gasped.

"The sight of space never gets old," said Amanda. "It's home."

Space seemed to go on forever. Though he was sure the pilot knew how to navigate this expanse, it seemed impossible. Each star looked like all the others.

Below them, Earth would be a tiny blue dot, the only solid point of reference. Just as he began to panic, a long silver tube surrounded by a slow-spinning ring at its center, came into view.

The shuttle glided closer, until the spindle filled the window, blocking out the blackness with something solid, something tangible. He wasn't sure when the actual connection happened as the only hint that they had docked was a soft whoosh at the same doorway where they'd entered. A loud click later, the door slid open to reveal a tube only slightly wider than the door itself.

"Come on," urged Amanda, already out of her seat. "You'll feel a little lighter than normal, but you'll get used to it quickly."

His steps did indeed feel like his feet barely touched the floor, perhaps due as much to elation as to the gravity. He knew he was grinning and that it marked him as a grounder, but he was too excited to care. He was on the spindle. In space.

The tube brought them to a small room with a bench along one side. Amanda sat. Alex took a spot beside her. He noticed a red light above the door blocking them from further access.

"Body scan," she informed him as though having a stranger view her every cell was no different than brushing her teeth.

Within moments, the light turned green. Amanda stood and the door opened. She gestured for him to follow.

His first few steps upon the actual spindle, with its row of narrow windows fully illustrating just how far from home he was, were uncertain. The gravity difference seemed to fade as he slowly tore his gaze from what he'd left behind to where he now walked. Beautiful people shared the wide plaza, passing by him without a second glance. Fantastical greenery towered in giant pots at regular intervals as far as he could see down the concourse. The lighting bore a bluish tint, not unpleasant, but lending Amanda's pale skin an almost glowing appearance. He wondered if she found sunlight odd compared to what she was used to.

He stuck close to her, dreading the thought of being separated and possibly lost in such a large, strange place. She took a turn to the right and jogged up a set of stairs. This brought them to a landing where a clear, round pod with an open door waited. She stepped in, standing aside to make room for him. They stood side by side as the door closed. The pod shot forward, or was it upward? Within seconds, Alex had lost his bearings. He stumbled forward, sure he was about to land face-first on the clearplaz of the pod. Amanda grabbed his arm and held him upright.

"Thanks."

She nodded.

The pod came to a gentle halt as quickly as it had launched, delivering them to another landing. People dressed in strange clothing in colors, and textures he'd never seen, milled about. A pair of them stepped into the pod he and Amanda vacated. Again, no one paid him any mind. If he was some sort of honored guest, it seemed no one recognized him.

Amanda walked at a brisk pace, allowing no time for questions. He'd lost track of the turns and direction in a matter of minutes, distracted by the people they passed, all beautiful, far more so than Amanda, who now seemed ordinary in comparison. They stood taller with thin elegant limbs and necks, their features near ethereal. He couldn't help but stare.

He came up short, almost running into Amanda when she stopped at a doorway. Similar to home, she activated the door panel. He followed her inside.

The suite was every bit as large as his apartment and furnished with a decadence he could never hope to afford. He stood in the middle of the foyer, taking it all in.

"This will be your room during your stay with us. I must ask that you stay here unless I'm with you. It's easy to get lost on the spindle."

He nodded. "All this space? It's for me? Alone?"

She smiled warmly. "For a few days. The bedroom is over there if you'd like to put your bag down. Our meal should arrive any minute."

Alex entered a bedroom twice the size of the one he shared with Emma. He set his bag on the long, low dresser and sat on the edge of the bed. Giving in to temptation, he fell backward onto a mattress that cradled his body until he felt weightless. Though he was more awake than he'd ever been, he couldn't wait to experience sleep here.

A pang of guilt hit him. If only Emma could have come with to see all this. He stared at the burnished gold glossy walls, brushed his hand over the thick silken comforter, and noted the pattern in the deep amber wood of the dresser, the invigorating scent of the air, and every other detail of the bedroom he could gather. When he got home, he'd tell Emma everything. No confidentiality agreement would convince him to keep all of this wonder to himself. Besides, what harm could there be in sharing details about the room where he stayed?

The sound of the suite door opening brought him to his feet. Amanda already had two covered rectangular trays on the table that could have easily seated six. She sat at one end and gestured for him to take the other. Following her lead, he pulled the cover off.

Steam and the aroma of the feast that awaited, instantly made his mouth water. Double portions of bacon and sausage sat beside scrambled eggs and a stack of the thickest pancakes he'd ever seen, dripping with syrup. Golden toast slathered in butter, crisp wedges of potatoes, and a bright assortment of sliced fruits sat alongside a large glass of orange juice and another of milk, condensation running down both glasses. He took a drink, surprised to find the milk ice cold despite being next to all the warm food. He'd sampled several blissful bites of everything before he remembered Amanda.

"Eat up," she said, slicing a delicate sliver from her pancakes, the only item on her tray other than a glass of water. "There is no dietary monitoring here. Nothing you do will count against you when you get home. You've worked all your life for this reward. Enjoy it."

Not needing to be told twice, Alex indulged himself in the abundance of food. It all tasted richer, so much better, like he was experiencing true flavor for the first time. His taste buds wept for joy.

Eventually, he put his fork down even though plenty of food remained. Two more people could have filled themselves from all he'd left behind. So wasteful, but Amanda didn't chide him for it. She'd left most of her pancakes too. He supposed that if she dined with spindle guests regularly, she couldn't gorge herself as he'd done or her figure would suffer for it.

"We should begin our tour so you'll have plenty of time to rest up before the big dinner tonight."

He rubbed his very satisfied stomach. "I don't think I could eat another thing until tomorrow."

Amanda laughed lightly. She covered both trays, leaving them on the table before walking to the door. "A walk will do you good, help your body digest all that."

"True." He fought off a yawn. With his stomach full, his out-of-whack sleep cycle was starting to catch up to him.

He stopped trying to keep track of where they were, instead focusing on sticking close to Amanda. When she halted next, he found they'd arrived at what appeared to be a medical facility.

"Why are we here?" he asked. While he was sure they had stunning technology given the apparent health of everyone he'd seen, he was far more interested in seeing the gardens or maybe a few stores. Past guests had mentioned those. He'd have to ask later about picking out souvenirs for Emma and the kids.

"Nothing to worry about. Like I said earlier, your health level is quite remarkable. The doctor would like to gather some samples from you. Nothing invasive, of course. What we learn could help the next generation of grounders to be more like you."

He'd never considered himself to be any better or different, but if he could help his children or grandchildren grow up healthier, a little poking and prodding would be well worth it.

"Sure."

"Thank you," said a man wearing a long-sleeved blue robe that covered him from neck to foot. If he had hair, it was hidden beneath a matching blue cap. His eyes were an even more striking blue. His thin lips drew into a smile. "If you'll just have a seat here."

Alex glanced at Amanda, who offered a reassuring nod as he sat on the examination table the doctor had indicated. Three nurses, moving so swiftly and dressed like the doctor that he couldn't tell if they were men or women, swarmed around him. One held his arm. Another drew blood. One snipped his hair then clipped two fingernails. The doctor examined his eyes and throat, then ran a scanner over his body. While he was distracted by holding still for the scanning wand, another needle pricked him in the back of his neck. The pain vanished a second later. Out of the corner of his eye, he caught sight of a long, thick needle and clear fluid in the syringe as the nurse stepped beside him to show it to the doctor. He nodded.

The flurry of activity came to a sudden halt, the nurses disappearing from view. The doctor stepped back to speak with Amanda before backing away.

"I hope that wasn't too much," Amanda said. "We do truly appreciate your assistance. Keeping the grounders in good health is very important to us."

"That's why you're here, the spindle, I mean."

Amanda nodded. "How are you feeling? No pain?"

He rubbed his arm and the back of his neck but realized he didn't have any discomfort despite all they'd done. "No. I feel fine."

"Wonderful." She nodded to the doctor as they left. "Now then, perhaps you'd like to see the gardens? We have a few hours to wait."

"Wait for what?"

"Your fitting. Guest of honor, remember?"

"Do I get to keep the new clothes when I go home?"

He couldn't wait to show off actual spindle clothing, stuff like he'd seen the people here wear.

"Oh yes."

Alex grinned. Amanda led him to one of the pod stations. He was better prepared for the motion this time. When they exited, a ten-minute walk brought him to the fantastic sight he'd been waiting for. The gardens spread out all around them, curving up the walls. Plants, from towering trees to spongy moss beneath his feet, awaited him. A rainbow of flowers dotted the grassy ground around the trees.

"May I touch them?"

"Of course." Amanda waved him into the garden, her smile every bit as indulgent as Emma's when the kids asked to play at the park. He supposed all grounders asked the same questions. Their excitement over things Amanda lived with every day must be wearing.

He left her behind, near running into the ferns that reached his waist, climbing over moss-covered boulders, and smelling flowers he'd only ever seen in projection copies of ancient books. There were only a few other people here and plenty of space to avoid them, to pretend he was alone in a peaceful forest. The sound of running water drew him to a trickling stream where tiny fish flashed through the water, dancing over the pebbles and darting through feathery deep green water plants. He laughed at the sheer joy of it all.

Amanda found him hours later, running his

fingers over the thirty-third different bark texture he'd found. "There are so many different kinds of trees," he said.

"Yes, the original grounder visitors brought samples from all over Earth. Most of these no longer exist anywhere on the ground." She nodded toward the exit. "We need to get back to your room. I'm sure you're ready for that nap by now."

Her mention of a nap brought on the wave of sleepiness he'd forgotten about since they'd left his room. He yawned. "That sounds wonderful. But what about the fitting?"

"Plenty of time for that later. Follow me."

Following would be easy. He could do that. Alex concentrated on keeping his drooping eyes open and staying within two steps of his guide. When she opened the door to his room, he shook his head, not quite remembering the pod ride back to this section of the spindle.

"I think I should sleep for a bit," he said, already heading for the comfortable bed he'd tested earlier.

"The fitters will stop by in a couple of hours. I'll see you for dinner later."

"Thanks for everything, Amanda."

"No problem at all. The pleasure is all mine. Sleep well."

Alex woke bleary-eyed and unsure how much time had passed. Had he missed his appointment with the fitters? Was he late for dinner? He tried to roll over to check the time display but discovered he couldn't move. And he wasn't in bed. Cold, hard metal registered on his back. Directly on his back. He was naked.

"It's awake," said the thing standing over him. "The nerve inhibitor patch will be fully active in...three, two, one."

It turned to face him. Not a thing, but one of the spindle dwellers wearing a clear hood and a red shiny suit that covered his entire body.

His cold blue eyes drilled into Alex as he bared his teeth. "You're going to be delicious. We have plans for every scrap, don't worry. None of you will go to waste."

Alex forgot how to breathe. He had to still be sleeping. This was a dream. Hell, the whole trip to the spindle could be a dream. Why would they pick him anyway? He tried to laugh, but he couldn't make a sound.

"Let me know when stability is confirmed. I'm ready to start carving the meat," the man standing over him called out.

"Activating the suit now," said a woman.

Alex tried to turn his head but could only strain his eyeballs to see another red-suited person at the other end of the white-tiled room. A hose with a sprayer wand hung from the ceiling off to his left. A cart lined with white trays and several containers was wheeled beside where he lay.

"How's the fit look?" asked the man beside him.

"Checking the primary responses."

"The chef can't wait to get started and I'm famished," said a familiar voice. Amanda. She stepped into his line of sight.

"Alex, meet your suit," she said.

Another set of footsteps drew closer. Alex stared up at himself. His doppelgänger's face bore no expression, no hint of the terror flooding through Alex's mind.

Amanda patted Alex's shoulder and put her other hand on the shoulder of the suit. "As per the agreement, your family will be taken care of, financial compensation and all of that. Your suit will make sure they suffer no emotional issues with your loss. We've copied everything. Don't worry, we've been doing this for generations, the transfer is flawless. Your family won't notice the difference."

"If only the grow team could replicate the flavor of the source material," said the man in the clear hood. "It would save us so much trouble."

"We're ready for the fitting," announced the woman at the other end of the room. "Bring Ari in."

"Yes, well, the hassle of wrangling the feeding stock does have its benefits. Like making the trash suffer," said Amanda.

She turned to Alex. "I told you, you're an honored guest. Most of you go back as empty suits."

Two tall men entered the white room holding the arms of a third. The third man, though an elegant spindle-dweller, he appeared disheveled. Bruises lined his face and his bare arms and chest. He wore only a pair of pants, his feet also bare on the plascrete floor. They came to a stop next to a grated floor drain.

"I'm innocent!" Ari yelled. "You can't do this!"

"Save it. You've been sentenced," said the woman. She held a metal wand to the base of his skull and pressed a button.

The man jerked, his body going stiff. The muscles in his neck and face stood out.

"You're going to kill me," he ground out between clenched teeth.

"Not permanently. You'll live out another seventy years or so. We chose one of the healthiest stock for you. We do care for our own."

Ari writhed in the grasp of his captors.

The woman removed the wand. Long wire-like tendrils retracted from Ari's body, vanishing into the wand. She set the device down and picked up another. With this one in hand, she came around him to press it to his forehead.

"Your body will be preserved. When this suit dies, you will be harvested before its disposal. You will be brought back to us and given the option to conform. Should you choose to do so, you will be returned to your own body and restored to your position. If, after seeing how the stock lives and thinks, after experiencing death, you still feel their lives are equal to ours, we will find you a new suit. The next one will not be as optimal. Your sentence will be repeated. Do you understand?"

He spat onto her clear-hooded face. Alex wished he could do the same.

"We seeded this world like the others. For over 100,000 years, we allowed them the rights and freedom you demand they deserve. You've seen what they did with what they were given." She shook her head inside the clear hood. "It's time they give back. Food is all they've proved they're good for."

"I'll find where we went wrong. We can learn from this. You'll see."

She activated the device on his forehead. It emitted a crackling noise and a bright pulse of light. Ari went limp. The men holding him let go. His body crumpled to the floor.

"Put that in containment. I have a feeling it will be a few lifetimes before we'll see Ari in person again." She picked up the wand and approached Alex's doppelgänger who was currently staring at the wall, seeming entirely unaffected by what had just transpired. With the wand placed against the base of his skull, she activated it.

The doppelgänger jerked like Ari had. A host of emotions ran over his face before settling on wide-eyed terror. He gasped and clutched his chest. "Something is wrong. It's so hard to breathe. I can't catch my breath.

"You'll get used to it," said the woman. She kept the device in place with one hand and ran a scanner wand over his head and chest with the other. After consulting the readings, she set the scanner aside. "Everything checks out. Their systems did not develop to our level of efficiency. As we've all told you, they are inferior."

"You're wrong," he said, lifting one arm awkwardly. After several attempts, he formed a fist.

"We're not. Farewell, Ari. I'm switching your control of the mind and body over to the suit now. May your sentence be fruitful." She pressed a series of buttons on the wand.

The arm lowered, the fingers relaxing. The doppelgänger's face went slack, his eyes half-lidded.

"Alex, how are you feeling?" Amanda asked the body Ari now inhabited somewhere deep inside.

"Strange. Am I dreaming?" he asked, his voice slurred.

"Yes. You'll wake up soon. We'll have dinner, and tomorrow you can go back to the garden for as long as you like. You'll be back with your family soon enough. Everything will be fine."

The red-suited woman extracted the device and nodded to Amanda. She led the suit out of the room.

Alex tried to struggle but still couldn't move. He

couldn't feel anything, not even the cold of the metal table.

"You may proceed," announced the woman.

"It's about damned time," muttered the man beside the table. He picked up a knife and sliced into Alex's leg.

The butcher set the first cut of meat on the tray. Inside his head, Alex could only scream.

About the Author

Jean Davis lives in West Michigan with her musical husband, two attention-craving terriers and a small flock of chickens and ducks. When not ruining fictional lives from the comfort of her writing chair, she can be found devouring books and sushi, weeding her flower garden, or picking up hundreds of sticks while attempting to avoid the abundant snake population that also shares her yard. She writes an array of speculative fiction.

Read her blog, *Discarded Darlings*, and sign up for her mailing list at www.jeandavisauthor. com. You can also follow her on Facebook and Instagram @JeanDavisAuthor, and on Goodreads and Amazon.